VISION

OF

MURDER

A Smiley and McBlythe Mystery

VISION

OF

MURDER

A Smiley and McBlythe Mystery

BRUCE
HAMMACK

1

———

A scream pierced the quiet of the waiting room. Heather dug her fingernails into the back of Jack's hand. More screams filtered down the hall from an exam room in the optometrist's office.

"That doesn't sound good," said Steve, who sat to her right.

Heather noticed Steve had dropped his folded white cane and searched for it with his feet. "A little more to your right."

Jack pried her claws from his hand and examined the divots. "Relax. She's probably one of those hysterical types. You're here for a simple eye exam. Nothing to worry about."

The screams caused those waiting to squirm in their seats as Steve retrieved his cane. "I can tell the difference between a scream caused by hysteria, grief, or pain. That's pain, and it's the real thing." He leaned forward and turned his head toward Jack. "The optometrist is your buddy. Go find out what's going on."

"No," said Heather, as she placed her hand on Jack's thigh. She considered the suddenness of her response and changed it. "If it's some sort of emergency, they don't need you getting in the way."

Steve leaned back in his chair. "She's right. If it's an emergency, we should let the pros handle it."

I

Minutes passed. The screams subsided, replaced with deep sobs. In addition, sharp, indistinguishable words filtered down the hall leading to the exam rooms. Heather leaned into Steve. "Can you make out what they're saying?"

"Accusations and threats of lawsuits. The woman sounds middle-age, perhaps the mother of the patient." He lifted his chin. "I hear sirens and an air horn."

Jack spoke up. "I don't hear anything."

"You will. They're getting louder."

Steve's prediction proved accurate. Firefighters filed past, followed by a duo whose sleeve patches identified them as EMTs from The Woodlands, Texas's ambulance service. A collapsible gurney followed a short time later.

Heather looked down and noticed she'd not only left indentations in the back of Jack's hand, but had brought tiny amounts of blood in a couple of spots. She reached into her purse and retrieved a fresh tissue. "Sorry I'm so uptight."

"What did she do?" asked Steve.

Jack dabbed his hand with the tissue. "This cat I'm dating has sharp claws. The screams scared her and the back of my hand caught the worst of it."

"That reminds me of the time I crept up on Maggie when she was drying a cast-iron skillet. I grabbed her right under the ribs and she let out a screech. That's the last time I pulled that stunt."

"You didn't duck fast enough?" asked Heather.

"She spun and put a lump on my knob that took two weeks to go away. There I was, laid out on the kitchen floor with her standing over me with a black skillet. When she realized what she'd done, she dropped the skillet. It landed in the worst place you can imagine."

Heather tried to subdue the mental image, but a snort broke through her determination not to laugh. The other waiting patients turned their heads and stared at her.

The squeak of wheels brought Heather's attention back to

the scene at hand. She expected to see an elderly patient, perhaps someone who'd fallen and broken a hip. Instead, a young woman was strapped to the gurney being wheeled toward the door. The skinny jeans, high-top designer tennis shoes, and Texas State University sweatshirt gave indications of a college-age student. She wore a bulbous gauze patch over her right eye as her body convulsed in sobs.

Following the gurney parade, a woman in her mid-forties strode past. Her face and neck were splotches of crimson and cream. She spun and pointed an accusatory finger at the man wearing a white lab coat. "Quit apologizing, and don't tell me I shouldn't call the police. My daughter walked in here with two good eyes and now…"

She spun and trotted to catch up without completing her thoughts.

The man on the receiving end of the woman's wrath was Chris Craddock, the optometrist who was to examine Heather's eyes. She recognized him from photos of a five-day cruise Jack and some of his buddies had taken out of Galveston. Buried in work, as usual, Heather missed out on the vacation. It worked out for the best because Steve needed her to help solve a murder. The cruise had turned into an all-guy trip for Jack and three others.

Chris took in a deep breath, let it out, and thrust his hands in the pockets of his lab coat. He stood as if not knowing what to do next.

Heather used the time of silence to note Dr. Craddock's physical appearance so she could relate the details to Steve—five feet, eleven inches, approximately 175 pounds, trim, neat appearance, expensive slacks and shoes, no visible scars or tattoos, and no wedding band.

"As I'm sure you're all aware," said Chris, "there's been an unfortunate incident here this morning. I'm sorry to inconvenience you, but the remainder of this morning's appointments are cancelled. Either myself or a member of the staff will call you and reschedule as soon as possible. To make up for the inconvenience, I'll reduce the charge for a standard appointment by twenty-five percent."

After he herded people out of the waiting room, Chris grabbed Jack by the sleeve of his shirt. "Bring Heather. We need to talk."

"Steve's here too. If it's all right, I'll bring him along."

"Is he the detective you're always talking about?"

Jack answered with a nod.

"Good. I may need a couple of top-notch private investigators and a talented lawyer. Let's go to my office and I'll tell you what happened."

Jack went over to Steve and Heather. "Chris wants to talk to us in his office."

Before they could take a step, a woman wearing a dark blue smock entered the office and ran into Chris's arms. "I came as soon as I could get away." The woman looked to be in her mid-twenties, but her demeanor and squealing voice made her seem younger, more like a thirteen-year-old at a concert.

Chris pushed her to arm's length. "Did you lock the store?"

"Not exactly. I put the closed sign on. What happened?"

Chris took a step back. "Sandi, go open the store. I don't have time to explain, we can't afford to lose any business today. I'm counting on you to sell glasses to everyone who walks through the door. Don't forget to up-sell a spare pair and sunglasses. I'll stop by and explain what happened before I go to lunch."

The woman pushed out her bottom lip, but nodded her acceptance of the assignment. Heather watched her walk toward the door. If Sandi's selling technique was half as good as her walk-away, Chris's business should be booming.

Heather shifted her gaze to the men in the room. Jack and Chris were still staring at the door. She cleared her throat and spoke, breaking Jack's focus. "Who was that?"

"That's Sandi Fields," said Chris. "She manages my retail

store next door. Well, not really mine; the bank and I are co-owners of the store and this office. I write the prescriptions then send the customers next door with a percentage-off coupon for their glasses. Sandi's the best eyeglass seller I've ever met. She flirts with the men and compliments the women. She's great with teenage girls, too."

Jack looked at the door and shook his head. "You have a model for an assistant, and I have my mother." He must have realized the thin ice he'd walked onto and cleared his throat. "Of course, I wouldn't trade Mom for the world. She's the best receptionist and office administrator I could hope for."

Heather gave Jack an exaggerated pat on the back. "Good tactical retreat."

Instead of going back to his office, Chris went to the door and threw the latch to lock it. "Now we can talk without being interrupted."

Steve held out his hand. "Hello, Chris, I'm Steve Smiley. Why don't you stop pacing and have a seat?" Steve returned to his chair and asked, "What caused that young woman to scream?"

Heather and Jack returned to their chairs and waited for Chris to join them. Instead, he continued to pace. "It was a routine eye exam that included dilating her eyes."

"What's her name?" asked Steve.

"Mattie Arnold. She's a sophomore at Texas State University. She's been my patient for years and is only a little far-sighted. Easily corrected with glasses or contacts. Like most girls her age, she wears contacts. Her mother has always been a bit of a helicopter parent, but we got along fine until today."

Jack interrupted. "Cut to the chase. Why all the screaming and the ambulance?"

Chris gave an exaggerated nod to his head. "I was getting to that. She came out of the chair when I put a dilating drop in her eye. I went into full emergency mode and irrigated her eye with water. It was quite the struggle. I don't know why she reacted so violently."

Steve uncrossed his legs. "You must have a theory."

"I've seen nothing like it in all my years of practice."

"Are you sure you administered the right drops?"

Chris thrust his right hand into the pocket of his lab coat. "I have the bottle right here. It's the correct label. We use this stuff every day and have never had a problem with it."

"Was Mattie your first patient of the day?" asked Steve.

"Yes."

Jack rubbed his chin. "I'm thinking like a defense attorney. If I remember the last time I came in for an exam when you dilated my eyes it stung a little, but soon went away. Is that right?"

"Yeah. The pain level should never exceed two or three."

"Was it a fresh bottle?"

"Now that you mention it, I don't recall. We keep it locked in a cabinet at night, but leave it out during the day."

"Who's 'we'?" asked Heather.

"Sorry, there is no 'we' at the current time. There used to be, but my assistant moved on. I haven't had time to hire a new one."

Jack took his turn. "Is there any chance the manufacturer made a bad batch of drops?"

Chris shrugged. "I guess anything's possible, but the controls they use are bulletproof."

Heather looked at Jack, and he returned her gaze.

Steve picked up the questioning where Jack left off. "Can you think of anyone who would like to see harm come to you or your practice?"

"Not really."

"What about disgruntled customers or an employee you let go recently?"

"No one stands out."

Jack piped up. "What about Melody?"

"Who's Melody?" asked Steve.

Jack answered for Chris. "The spurned ex-wife. A messy divorce resulted in Melody getting the kids, the house, the—"

Chris spat out the rest of the list. "She also took over my practice and got the best dog I'll ever own. She's a cat person, so go figure." He cocked his head. "Why did you say you're thinking like an attorney?"

"Something bad happened here today, and the girl's mother likely wants a head as a souvenir. I can almost smell a lawsuit."

Steve added, "I don't want to worry you unnecessarily, but it would be wise to talk to an attorney and start planning a strategy on how to handle this."

Heather added, "Expect a thorough investigation. Criminal and civil."

The words had no more left her mouth when a series of sharp knocks sounded. Chris looked at Jack and raised his eyebrows.

Steve puffed out his cheeks. "That will be the police. You'd better open up and get this over with."

2

———————

Heather looked on as a vaguely familiar man entered the waiting room wearing a nice, but off-the-rack sports coat and slacks. "Are you Dr. Christopher Craddock?" The man showed his badge and identification.

"Yes."

Steve stood. "Detective Hall, is that you?"

The detective sidestepped Chris to get a look at who'd called him by name. "It's Steve Smiley and his partner, Heather McBlythe. I thought you two only worked homicides."

Steve and the detective took steps toward each other as Hall acknowledged Heather with a guarded smile and a nod.

It took Heather a few extra seconds to recognize the detective, probably because he'd shaved his mustache and reduced the hair on his head to nothing but short stubble. Hall and his then-partner were assigned to investigate the first case she and her blind mentor worked together—the murder of Steve's former college roommate, Ned Logan. The success of solving that case led her and Steve to form their investigation partnership.

After the brief reunion, Hall got down to business. "We received a phone call about an incident that occurred earlier this morning. It seems a young woman came for an exam and left with damage to her eye. What can you tell me about that, Dr. Craddock?"

Jack spoke up by introducing himself as Chris's attorney.

"I'm not here to arrest anyone" said Hall in an even voice. "This is a preliminary investigation where we take statements from witnesses."

"I'll need to consult with my client in private first."

Chris raised an open hand toward the hall. "We can use my office."

Steve took a step toward Detective Hall. "Why don't you ask Heather and me your questions? She can tell you what she saw and heard. I'm good at details about what I heard. Then we can both tell you what Dr. Craddock told us."

"That sounds like a good start. It will also give me time to talk to the receptionist." He looked at Jack. "If I hear anything that rises to a crime, and your client is involved, things could change fast."

Jack nodded.

The optometrist and the attorney walked out of the lobby and shut the door behind them.

Steve launched into a detailed account of what he'd heard. Heather added details of what she'd seen and heard. Steve took over again and added a detail or two of what Chris told them.

After scribbling notes, Hall looked up from his notebook. "Where's the bottle of eye drops?"

Steve shrugged. "You'll need to ask Dr. Craddock when he and Jack return."

Heather and Steve sat side-by-side as Hall interviewed the receptionist. It didn't take long, and his questions ended as Chris and Jack returned to the waiting room.

"Where's the bottle of eye drops?" asked Hall.

Chris reached into the pocket of his lab coat and took out the bottle. "Right here."

Hall reached out with a plastic evidence bag and motioned

for Chris to place the plastic bottle in it. "I'll have this analyzed and let you know what we find."

Jack spoke up. "After consulting with my client, we've concluded it was a tragic incident, most likely caused by either a manufacturing error or someone tampering with the bottle prior to its arrival at this clinic. Either way, Dr. Craddock is beyond suspicion."

"You're probably right, but that's not stopping the girl's parents from making accusations." Detective Hall shifted his attention to Steve. "Good to see you again, Steve, and you too, Heather."

After the door closed behind the detective, Chris looked around the empty waiting room. "That puts an end to my morning appointments. How does a late breakfast sound? There's a deli down the block with great coffee and pastries, or sandwiches and salads if you're ready for an early lunch."

"Sounds good. My treat," said Heather.

Steve took a step toward the door. "Free food has always been my favorite kind."

Jack guided Heather with his hand on her elbow. She took a last look down the hallway leading to the exam rooms and breathed a sigh of relief.

"You three go ahead," said Chris. "I'll tell the receptionist where I'm going and have her reschedule patients."

Heather asked, "Don't you need to stop at the retail shop and tell Sandi what happened?"

Chris dismissed the question with a flip of his wrist. "She can wait."

***

THE SHORT MAN BEHIND THE COUNTER WORE A YARMULKE and spoke with a heavy accent. His appearance and voice inflections, along with the heady smell of fresh-baked bread, brought back Heather's memories of the mom-and-pop delis scattered throughout Boston. So strong were the memories that she abandoned her carb-free, mostly vegetarian diet and ordered a blueberry scone. She made a commitment to spend an extra twenty minutes on the treadmill at the gym to justify the splurge.

By the time Steve and Jack placed their orders, Chris arrived, hollered at the man behind the counter to give him the usual, and joined the trio. "What a lousy morning. The one thing I didn't need was to lose half a day's income."

Jack asked, "Is money still tight?"

"Tight is an understatement." He sighed. "To tell the truth, it's my fault. After Melody cleaned me out, I thought I could start over on the same scale. The clinic, the separate retail store, hiring staff, and buying equipment. It all took more than I counted on."

Heather had heard a version of the same story a thousand times. Companies tried to build too fast. Many would overestimate income and not realize the true cost of everything needed to open and operate a successful business. Financial stress led to ulcers, burnout, ruptured relationships, desperate attempts to hang on, and eventual bankruptcies. It happened all too often to businesses, large and small.

She tuned back in to the conversation as Chris flashed a smile. "Oh, well. You only live once. Might as well swing for the fences while I'm still young enough to enjoy life."

Chris turned to face Heather. "Correct me if I'm wrong, but I sensed you didn't feel comfortable being in my waiting room today. Was there something about it that bothered you? I tried really hard to make it a casual, welcoming space."

While she tried to maintain a blank countenance, Heather's stomach did a slow roll. "Your waiting room is one of the most attractive I've ever been in."

"But?"

Heather searched for words that didn't come, so Steve answered for her. "She hates medical, dental, and eye exams."

Chris nodded. "That's more common than most people realize. Everyone deals with fear."

"I'd say it's a dislike of waiting more than fear," countered Heather.

"I was right on schedule today. If you waited over five minutes, it's because you arrived early."

Jack tilted his head. "He's got you there. I noticed the muscles in your shoulders felt like rocks as we walked into the building. Chris is right. Something sets you off when you go to an appointment about your health."

Heather tried not to make her words sound curt. "Let's get back to the matter at hand. What are you going to do to help Chris?"

Jack leaned back. "Nothing for now, except advise him not to talk to the press if they call."

"Press?" Chris's eyes widened. "Why would the press be interested in me? You said it was most likely a mistake made by the manufacturer."

Jack chuckled. "Truth is often the first casualty of the press and the legal system. Also, look at the victim—a cute college girl with her life suddenly altered." Jack took a breath. "When we get back to your office, I'll write a statement you can give. It will shift suspicion away from you."

Chris's gaze went to a window overlooking the parking lot. "I wonder how much business this will cost me."

Steve spoke up. "You'd better pray a big news story involving someone else breaks today."

"That's not very encouraging."

Silence settled over the table. Steve broke it by saying, "Tell us about your employees."

"What do you want to know?"

"It surprised me to hear you put the drops in Mattie Arnold's eyes this morning. Isn't that the job of an assistant?"

"It should have been, but like I said earlier, it's only me and the receptionist now. She's a temp and doesn't know anything about optometry. In a strange way, I looked forward to doing everything myself. It reminds me of how things were when I opened my first practice."

"Tell us what that was like," said Heather.

"Simple. Melody, my ex-wife, was the receptionist, and I did everything else." He looked away. "We leased a small building for the practice. She found used equipment at a discount price. We didn't have a retail store then. They were good days." He brought his gaze back to those at the table. "Clocks only run forward. I need to think about the future, not dwell on the past."

Further discussion had to wait as the owner delivered their orders and regaled them with details of the quality ingredients he used to craft his masterpieces. Heather had to admit the scone matched anything she'd had in Boston, even though the atmosphere wasn't the same.

Between bites, Jack wiped crumbs from the corner of his mouth. "How long has Sandi Fields worked for you?"

Chris looked up at the ceiling. "At least four... make that five, years."

"That means she worked for you a long time before you and Melody divorced."

Chris nodded and talked around a bite. "When we split, Sandi wanted to come with me. It made Melody furious, but I knew I couldn't make ends meet without Sandi selling like she does." He put down his fork. "She may look and talk like a dumb blond, but she's a selling machine. Most retail stores carry frames for glasses in all price ranges, because they cater to a wide variety of customers. Sandi only orders frames with designer names. Bigger mark-up, bigger profit. There's a bunch of other techniques she uses to make sure we get the maximum profit from each customer."

Heather chased a bite with a swig of coffee and placed her fingertips on the table while looking at Chris. She opened her mouth to speak, but then looked down at what remained of her scone.

"What did you want to ask me?"

"This may be my imagination, but it looked like Sandi has designs on your future that include her. Am I wrong?"

"Probably not." He took another bite and held up a finger, showing he had something else to say. "She played it cool around Melody, but that changed after Mel put my belongings in the front yard and had the locks changed. Sandi and I had a brief fling, but it meant nothing to me."

Steve spoke up again. "Was the fling before or after Melody cleaned out your closet?"

"After. My attorney wasn't very good, but I did heed her advice and behaved myself until after the divorce."

Jack lifted the last bite from his plate but didn't raise it to his mouth. "I know the attorney that represented you. The only reason you got such a raw deal is that you agreed to everything Melody's attorney hit you with."

"I didn't want Mel or the kids to suffer."

Jack mumbled something under his breath and popped the last bite into his mouth.

Heather considered the man who should have examined her eyes. Chris was a walking contradiction. On the one hand, he had grandiose ideas about running a business, but he spoke with fondness about the early days when life boiled down to a man, a woman, and a small practice. He openly admitted to a dalliance with an employee, but not until a judge ordered the marriage bonds severed. Now, he's on the precipice of financial ruin, the product of his own doing. Yet, he presents himself as a likable, smart, and competent professional. She wondered about his ex-wife. What type of woman was Melody? She also wondered if marriage was worth it if a nice guy like Chris couldn't make it work?

"Heather," said Jack. "Where did you go?"

"Oh, sorry. My mind was a million miles away."

"Another big deal to close?"

"Not any time soon. I'm focused on an existing big deal that might fall through."

"I better get back and see how the receptionist is doing on those phone calls," said Chris.

The four of them rose in unison. Once outside the deli, Jack released Heather's hand. "Hold up, Chris."

"What is it?" asked Steve.

"There's a television remote broadcast truck parked in front of Chris's building." Jack turned to face Chris. "Take Steve back in the deli while Heather and I get her SUV. You need to call your office and cancel your afternoon appointments too."

"I can't afford to do that."

"Trust me on this. If a reporter gets you on camera today, you're out of business."

"He's right," said Steve. "Instead of taking me back in the deli, take me to the business next door. People in the press live on coffee."

"But it's a bridal shop."

"Perfect. They'll never look for you there."

3

———

The sound of Heather's new Mercedes SUV leaving their condo complex accompanied that of children frolicking in the pool of the gated community. The peals of joy lay far enough away that Steve heard only the shrillest squeals. He punched in the code to unlock his front door and stepped into what he considered the most important invention of the twentieth century—central air conditioning.

He stood his white cane by the door. No need to carry it around the two-bedroom condo, as he had the layout and obstacles memorized. The plastic flap to the pet door slapped open. Max, Heather's Maine Coon cat, meowed as he rubbed his head on Steve's leg. It was past treat time and the pestering wouldn't stop until the bottom of Max's bowl was covered.

"Hey, buddy. What will it be? Do you want canned food or some of those ocean-flavored dry snacks?"

Max replied with a double meow.

"No, you can't have both." Steve went to the pantry, retrieved a new packet of treats and trickled them into Max's bowl. After placing it on a plastic mat on the kitchen floor, Steve ran his hand down the pudgy cat's back, marveling once more at how much Max's fur felt like sable. He then strode to the living room and assumed his usual position in his recliner. Before long, Max made himself at home on Steve's lap.

With nothing on Steve's agenda for the rest of the day, he stroked Max, listened to baritone purrs, and began a one-sided conversation. "Max, did you know Heather's afraid of having her eyes examined? In fact, she's afraid of all exams. You've known her longer than me. Why is she such a scaredy-cat?"

Purrrr.

"She needs an exam 'cause she's getting headaches and her ability to read fine print isn't what it used to be. Going to any kind of doctor is a genuine fear for Heather. That's why Jack and I went with her today." Max tilted his head as Steve scratched his ear. "Her fear of medical exams doesn't make sense, but I guess everyone is afraid of something."

Steve stroked the soft fur from head to tail. "Speaking of medical appointments, let me tell you what happened at the optometrist's office today."

He recounted the morning's experience and used it to make a couple of points. "First, we have the young lady named Mattie Arnold. She's afraid of permanent damage, and rightfully so. But I'm sure it doesn't stop there. A young girl like her is probably afraid people will ridicule her if she loses sight in her eye, and that her friends will shun her. More than that, I bet she's afraid no young man would want to date her, let alone marry her."

Max lowered his head to Steve's chest.

"Then there's her mother. Her fear came out as anger and she directed it at Dr. Craddock." Steve kept stroking, and Max continued to purr. "I know she shouldn't have called the television station, but fearful people do things they wouldn't normally do."

Steve remained silent for several seconds. "What's that, Max? What am I afraid of?" He paused. "I haven't given that question much thought lately. I realized my worst fears when those thugs attacked Maggie and she died."

He stroked Max's fur in silent contemplation. "Am I afraid of dying? No, not anymore. Don't get me wrong. I'm not trying to rush it, like I once wanted to, but I'll take it without complaint when it comes."

The announcement of an incoming call from Kate Bridges put the philosophical discussion on the back burner.

"Hello, Kate. This is a pleasant surprise."

"I hope I didn't catch you at a bad time."

"Not at all. Max and I were discussing fear. So far, it's been one-sided."

Kate chuckled. "It's good to know I'm not the only person who discusses the deep mysteries of life with things that can't talk back. For me it's the characters in my novels. Now that I think about it, they're my favorite therapists."

"They're certainly worth what we pay them, which is more than I can say for some of the two-legged ones." Steve paused. "It's good to hear from you. I've been meaning to call, but now that I think about it, I was afraid to."

"You, afraid? Hard to believe. Why would you be afraid to call me?"

Steve took in a deep breath. "I can't find the motivation to continue writing short stories. I listen to what I've written and they sound like a third grader dictated them."

"What you're experiencing is called imposter syndrome. It's the false belief that we don't have good stories to tell and we lack the skill to tell them. Almost every writer I know experiences it, especially the unpublished ones."

"What's the cure?"

"Don't quit."

Steve scratched his chin. "That's all there is to curing imposter syndrome?"

"That's the most important thing. As an experienced editor, I'd also say you need to put more emotion into your stories."

"Where have I heard that before?"

Kate laughed. "The same place you'll keep hearing it from until you do it."

Steve lowered his voice. "Does this mean we're going back to our previous arrangement?"

"If you can stand my ruthless critiques of your stories, then the answer is yes."

"Kate, you're a God send."

"Same to you."

An awkward few seconds of silence followed. Steve cleared his throat. "Let me tell you what happened this morning at an optometrist's office. I think there may be a good short story in it if I can capture some of the emotion."

For the next hour, they talked about writing.

HEATHER ARRIVED AT HER CONDO A LITTLE AFTER SIX IN THE evening. It seemed odd to drive home before the evening sun called it a day, but she wanted a warm shower, loose clothes, and a conversation with someone who didn't want to tell her how to run her life. She accomplished the first two items on her mental list of things to do and went next door for the third.

She punched the key code into Steve's door lock and stuck her head inside his condo. "Are you busy?" She saw the top two inches of Steve's head as he sat in his recliner. He raised a hand and motioned her to enter. "Come in. Max and I are watching reruns of a senate confirmation hearing."

She shuffled in barefooted and plopped down on the couch next to Steve's chair. "You might as well watch paint dry. Isn't there something more interesting on?"

"I'm keeping in practice."

Heather shook her head in disbelief. "In practice for what?"

"Detecting lies. If you want to buy a couch, go to a furniture store. If you want to study lies and deception, this is the program to listen to."

"You never cease to amaze me." Heather stood. "What do you want for supper?"

"Max wants sushi. That sounds good to me, too."

"Yum. I'll order it. Do you want your usual?"

"You guessed it."

After she placed the order, Heather fed Max his reduced ration of who-knows-what in a pull-top tin. She returned to the couch, and all but fell onto it.

"You must've had a bad day. I can always tell by how you sit."

She issued a sigh of lament. "Jack and I had words this afternoon. I'm not sure Chris is a good influence on him."

"Oh?"

She'd heard Steve ask this simple question at least a hundred times. It meant she could go on and explain the argument if she wanted to talk. If she didn't, she could sidestep the issue. It was time to talk. "After we dropped you off, those two ganged up on me about being afraid of having my eyes examined."

"And you said?"

"That I'd be crazy not to be afraid after what happened to Mattie Arnold. That didn't satisfy either of them. They kept badgering me as if they were psychoanalysts. I kept my cool, but called Jack later and gave him a rather large piece of my mind."

Steve rubbed his chin. "Ah."

Heather's frustration bubbled over. "There you go again. 'Oh' and 'Ah.' Are those your favorite words?"

"They're the safest I've found when dealing with someone who's looking for another verbal boxing match. How did things end with Jack?"

She looked at Steve to tell him what she'd said, and how they'd traded jabs over the phone. The desire to relate their schoolyard barbs melted away when she saw the corners of Steve's mouth pull upward. The issue wasn't one of right or wrong; it had to do with maturity. At that moment, acting like a responsible adult wasn't on her radar.

She stuck her tongue out at Steve, and he returned the gesture. How he knew to mimic her actions was a mystery, but it always brought the same result. Both called a truce by laughing and moved on.

"Did you have a good day at the office? Any new big deals?" Steve asked.

Heather sensed the ground of business gave her a firmer footing than that of romantic relationships and psychoanalysis. "There are always a few deals on the burner, but nothing significant to report yet. The usual delays with the projects on Lake LBJ, and we're not making progress as fast as I'd like in Belize. I guess that's to be expected. I've been told the unofficial motto of that country is *Slow Down*. It's great for an advertising gimmick, but not so much when you're dealing with banks, government agencies, and construction deadlines."

"Perhaps you and Jack need to take another trip to Belize. The last time you went, you both came back in a great mood." Steve snapped his fingers. "Here's a better idea. Find a nice catamaran, take a week or two to sail there, and check out the construction progress when you arrive."

"A week or two? I can't be gone for more than two days, let alone a week."

"A week? You'll need that long just to slow down enough to where you can enjoy the trip. Then work a day or two, play for five days and fly home."

"Do you expect me to sail all the way to Central America?"

"I thought you blue bloods out of Boston know how to sail."

"Of course, I can sail. Let's say we rented a boat. Why wouldn't I sail it back to Galveston?"

"Rent? You're the one who's always looking for a bargain. Find a great deal on a boat, sail it to Belize, and sell it for a profit."

Heather's laugh came out in an unladylike snort. "That sounds like something you should work into the plot of one of your stories."

Steve leaned back. "Speaking of stories. Kate called me today."

Heather shifted to see if she could catch any nuance to his voice or posture. His voice did have a lift in it that wasn't there earlier in the day. "What did she have to say?"

"We talked for an hour. She agreed to help me with my writing again."

Heather pushed her palms together with fingers pointed heavenward. She mouthed a silent, "Thank you, Lord."

Steve kept talking. "Don't get any ideas. She's my writing coach. That's all."

Steve could say what he liked. She knew his usual phone calls lasted only long enough for information to pass back and forth, and not a minute longer. For him to talk to Kate for an hour bordered on a miracle. She also knew his deceased wife, Maggie, still held a grip on his heart that might never go away. Best not to rush him, or he'd be like a bashful turtle and draw his head back into his shell. This would require her walking a fine line and showing the right amount of interest without pressuring him.

"When does she think your first short story will be ready to publish?"

He laughed. "First I have to discover emotion and not make the stories sound like the police reports I used to write."

"The emotion's already there. You proved it with the sailboat story you spun. Put a hint of romance in your murder stories and you'll be a best-selling author in no time."

A knock on the door put a temporary end to talk of Steve's renewed relationship with Kate, her rocky day with Jack and Chris, sailing away into the worry-free waters of the Caribbean, and Steve becoming a famous author.

The delivery driver had iridescent blue hair, along with piercings in his nose, eyebrows, and lower lip. Heather took the sack of sushi and cartons of fried rice. She turned and hollered. "Do you have cash for a tip?"

Steve stood, drew a ten-dollar bill from the front pocket of his shorts, and held it out for Heather to give to the young man.

"Thanks. This is almost enough to get my little girl a new pair of shoes."

Heather wished she'd brought her purse with her. She wondered why Steve didn't dig deeper, but dismissed it.

Once the door closed, she expressed the need to carry cash with her at all times.

Steve waved away her words. "I wouldn't worry about that young man. He used the same line about shoes for his daughter the last time Max and I ate sushi."

Heather tented her hands on her hips. "Do you mean he was lying?"

Steve shrugged. "He's working an angle. Sometimes you can't tell, but he gave himself away by repeating the same shoe story. Sort of like what Chris told us about only carrying designer frames. I bet there's some cheap ones somewhere in the store. He's desperate for sales. It's difficult to find the line between earning an honest living and putting a thumb on the scales to increase profits. I determined how much tip to give that driver the first time he delivered here. I'm not changing it until he stops playing the sympathy card. Ten bucks. No more, no less."

Heather placed the sticky rice rolls stuffed with all manner of goodies on plates. They sat at the dining room table to eat and talk about the day. She had chopsticks in hand when her phone alerted her to an incoming text. She swiped the screen and pushed the icon.

"Jack's on his way to the emergency room." She dropped the chopsticks. "His mother's having chest pains."

4

One of Heather's dropped chop sticks hit the side of the plate, rolled off the table, and fell to the floor as she shot from her chair. "Are you coming with me?"

"I'd only slow you down. Don't forget to take your phone, a charging cord, and your purse."

She spoke over her shoulder. "I'll text you when I know something."

In less than three minutes, she'd changed, collected everything she needed for a long night, and was backing out of her garage. Familiar landmarks on northbound I-45 came and went in a blur as she pressed her luck with the speed limit. It seemed like half an eternity passed before she wheeled into a parking space outside the hospital's emergency room. It wasn't until she jogged past Jack's Camaro that she recognized his car.

Doors slid open with a swishing sound as she entered a room with lights that seemed too bright. Jack's face was etched with worry lines. He hugged her with an intensity she'd never felt from him.

Heather had enough breath to whisper, "How is she?"

He kept hugging. "All they'll tell me is she's awake and answering questions."

Their hands found each other's as they took a half-step back.

"That sounds positive." Heather made a point of putting a reassuring tone to her words.

Jack's chin quivered, so she led him to a pair of chairs away from other people waiting. He took a deep breath and let it ease out. "I can't remember Mom ever being sick enough to go to the hospital." He looked around the room. "Nothing has changed since they brought Dad here."

Heather massaged the back of his hand with her thumb.

He looked into her eyes with renewed worry. "Dad went from a treatment room in this ER to the funeral home. I never got to tell him what I should have."

She needed to get his mind back on a positive track before it ended up in a ditch of despair. Turning in her seat, she faced him. "You listen to me, Jack Blackstock. Tonight is different from that night five years ago. Your mother is not your father, and you don't know yet what's going on with her or how serious it is."

His chin rested on his chest.

Heather kept talking. "I'm here for you."

Jack lifted his head and stared into her eyes. "Thank you. You don't know how much that means to me."

She twisted back to where she could see the room's occupants. They looked to be a sample from a pollster with every size, color, age, and socio-economic group represented. The thought occurred to Heather that illness and accidents don't discriminate.

She glanced at Jack and realized he'd fixed his gaze on the door leading to the ER. "Hey, handsome. I'm over here."

Jack turned and offered the first smile of the night. "Hey, gorgeous."

"Wait until you hear what Steve came up with tonight."

"Tell me."

She snuggled next to him. "He thinks it would be a good idea if I bought a catamaran and you and I sailed it to Belize."

Jack's cheeks lifted as he smiled. "That's the best idea I've ever heard."

Heather launched into the full account of the evening's conversation with Steve. She left nothing out, including his phone conversation with Kate. The better part of an hour passed before Jack looked at the door leading to the treatment rooms.

By that time, he'd regained his emotional balance enough to say, "Leave it to Steve to come up with a plan for you that includes work and pleasure."

"Did you eat supper?"

"Yeah. What about you?"

"One bite of a California roll. Steve probably put the rest of my order in the fridge."

"Or gave it to Max."

"He'd better not." She patted Jack on the hand. "I need a snack and coffee. What about you?"

"Only coffee. There's no telling how many tests they'll run or how long we'll be here."

"I brought my phone charger if you need it."

Jack pulled out his phone. "I'm down to twenty percent, and I need to update some people."

Heather handed him the cord before she went in search of the cafeteria. She returned twenty minutes later with two cups of black coffee in environmentally friendly paper containers.

"You weren't gone long. Did you find something to eat?"

Heather handed him one cup. "A yogurt parfait and an energy bar. The serving line closed at seven. Any word on your mom?"

"A nurse came out and said she's doing fine and isn't having any more pain. They're running tests on her but won't know what's wrong until they get the results."

"That sounds positive."

Jack crossed his fingers and held up his hands. "Now we wait and hope a string of ambulances doesn't arrive. So far, it doesn't seem like a busy night."

An hour later, Heather rested her head on Jack's chest. "You got your wish about no ambulances, but you forgot to mention walk-in patients." She looked around the crowded waiting area.

Jack's chest expanded and then contracted as he spoke. "This may take all night. Why don't you go home and get some sleep? I'll text you when I hear something."

"I have a better idea." She leaned away from him. "Consider what you'd do if our roles were reversed."

"I guess that means you're staying."

"Save my seat. I need to stretch my legs and get some fresh air."

Jack rose with her. "I'll tell the woman doing admissions we'll be outside."

A swarm of bugs congregated under the bright lights of the entrance, so Jack suggested they move away from the building. They stopped one row deep into the parked cars and faced the emergency room door, just in case. Once there, they both stretched, yawned, and groaned. Jack gave voice to the thought going through Heather's mind. "When did I get so old that sitting in a chair for a few hours makes my bones ache?"

"I need to get back to the gym and find a better yoga class," said Heather.

Jack chuckled. "Did I tell you I tried yoga on the cruise ship?"

"You? Yoga? I hope there's a photo to prove your claim, counselor."

"Two of us took the class. Chris told us he and Melody used to take classes together. He still takes the time every morning to do thirty minutes in the living room. Anyway, one thing led to another and the next thing you know, I'm on a thin mat in the ship's exercise room with an instructor in her twenties, limber as a gummy worm. My buddy and I laughed until we cried trying to get into and hold those positions."

"Chris didn't join you?"

Jack shook his head. "He didn't want to spend the extra money."

Heather swatted away a June bug that landed on her shoulder. "You never went into detail about that cruise. I guess you four lived it up."

"Mark Twain once said, 'Rumors of my death have been greatly exaggerated.' You can say the same thing about what we did on the cruise. To begin with, the four of us bunked two to a room. Inside cabins, the cheapest on the ship. Two twin beds, and a tiny bathroom. Even after trimming the cost of the cruise down to the bone, we had to cut a deal with Chris on the price so he could afford to go."

"What kind of deal?"

"Three of us split the cost of the two cabins. Chris promised to pay us back."

Heather shook her head. "That doesn't sound like something four successful men would do."

Jack shrugged. "We wanted him to come. The three of us went cheap and Chris was the miser."

"No drink package? How did Chris get the courage to talk to women?"

"Chris doesn't drink alcohol."

"No excursions or specialty dining?"

"He stayed on the ship and only ate in the main dining room, the buffet, and the other restaurants with complimentary food. We all decided before we left that we'd try to outdo each other by not spending on things that weren't included. It was a game." Jack issued an elfish grin. "I couldn't resist the yoga class after my buddy said I was afraid to try."

Jack stifled a yawn. "As a payback for us covering Chris's share of the cabin, he made trips to the buffet and brought us breakfast in bed every morning."

"I'm surprised he didn't have a room of his own so he could sow some more wild oats."

"Chris isn't as bad as you think he is."

"What about that fling he admitted to with Sandi Fields?"

Jack shook his head. "That was a one-and-done. You saw the way he got rid of her today."

"If Chris is such a saint, why did he divorce?"

Jack looked up at the stars and an almost full moon. "I never said he was a saint, and he never told me the unabridged story of the divorce. I'm pretty sure it had to do with money and the stress associated with trying to grow their business too fast. He and Melody weren't on the same page with their business plan and it cost them a good marriage."

A woman in scrubs appeared at the door and motioned for them to return. They took off at a trot.

"No need to rush," said the nurse as they approached. "Your mother is doing fine. In fact, she's been asleep for the past hour. Dr. Rosenberg ordered her discharge."

The nurse walked at a good clip, waved her badge in front of a card reader, and the wide door leading to the treatment rooms swung open. Heather expected to see people scurrying about like ants on a disturbed mound. Instead, the halls appeared empty, with only the sound of the occasional mechanical device breaking the quiet. The nurse pushed open a door and gestured for them to enter a room. Cora Blackstock lay in a bed with her head elevated. The top of a standard blue hospital gown peeked out from under a white sheet and blanket.

At the sight of the couple, she held out a hand for Heather to take. "Please tell me you haven't been waiting all this time."

Jack answered for her. "I tried to get her to go home, but she's as stubborn as you are."

Heather ignored him. "The nurse said you're being released. That's wonderful."

Cora winked. "That's what they do with people who aren't sick."

A voice came from over Heather's shoulder. "I told her she wasn't sick enough to stay here, but that doesn't mean she can leave and get a double cheeseburger, fries, and a milkshake."

The woman wearing the white lab coat turned her attention to Heather. "You must be Jack's wife. I'm Dr. Rosenberg."

Jack broke in before Heather could correct the doctor's mistake of her marital status. "This is Heather."

The omission of her last name made her breath catch. Did Jack do that on purpose? If so, they'd have to have a repeat of their talk about taking things slow.

Jack's next sentence ran into the last without him taking a breath. "What's the diagnosis?"

"Angina pectoris. Also known as stable angina, which in plain language is pain localized to the heart. There are at least fifteen potential causes for the sudden onset of chest pain. Some are as simple as exercising too strenuously or lifting too much. Others can be life threatening. Fortunately, we ruled out a heart attack, and X-rays show clear lungs and no enlarged heart. The electrocardiogram was within normal limits."

"See," said Cora. "I told you there's nothing wrong with me. Just a spell that came and went."

The doctor's collar-length raven hair moved side to side. "It's common for women in their sixties to minimize angina." The doctor turned and addressed Jack. "Based on the results of blood tests, there are some things that concern me, especially the cholesterol levels. I'm referring her to a cardiologist who will order other tests and get to the bottom of these sudden attacks of chest pain."

Heather spoke up. "Did you say attacks, as in plural?"

Jack fixed a narrow gaze on his mother. "Mom, how long has this been going on?"

The doctor held up a hand. "Save that question for later. Right now, I have other patients waiting and your mother doesn't need her attorney son cross-examining her."

Heather asked a one-word question. "Prognosis?"

The doctor smiled. "I like the way you ask questions. There's no immediate risk that I can see, but that doesn't mean she's in the clear. I'm recommending a modified diet, only light exercise, and a couple of prescriptions. She's leaving tonight with a small bottle of nitroglycerin tablets. If there's a recurrence of severe chest pain, place one tablet under the tongue and call EMS. Nitroglycerin will cause her blood pressure to drop almost immediately, which, by the way, is elevated. Make sure she carries the bottle with her at all times. I'm also prescribing a drug to help lower her bad cholesterol. The cardiologist may want to put her on a blood thinner, but I'll leave that decision to them. Expect a stress test along with another echo-cardiogram." She took a breath. "Questions? No? All right, then. She can get dressed."

The nurse opened the door for the doctor, closed it halfway again and turned back to them. "Don't get in a rush. Discharging takes twice as long as admitting. I'll come get you as soon as I can."

Heather looked at Jack. "Wait outside the door. I'll help her get dressed."

"You needn't do that. I feel fine now."

"No arguments. Jack would sue me for all I'm worth if I allowed you to fall in the treatment room of a hospital."

Cora giggled like a schoolgirl. "He just might."

On the way home from the hospital, Heather wondered how long it would be before she received a phone call summoning her to come to a hospital in Boston to attend to one of her parents. Days? Months? Years? She'd better call... just to check in.

5

―――――

Heather looked into two green eyes that blinked back at her. She tried to reach out and stroke her bedmate, but the tangled sheets made her into something of an Egyptian mummy. After breaking free, she gave Max a thorough scratch under his chin and behind the ears.

"What time is it?"

Since Max didn't answer, she rolled over and looked at the clock on her nightstand. "Good grief. It's twelve thirty. I've slept through half the day." She reached for her phone, intending to call her office. "Double good grief. I forgot to plug it in this morning after I called Mother." She looked again at her nightstand but didn't see the cord. Then she realized Jack used it at the hospital and had stuffed it into the pocket of his slacks.

Heather sighed. "That's what I get for being clutter-averse. I should've heeded Steve's advice to get a spare."

With teeth brushed, wearing leggings and a T-shirt, she pushed open the pet door that connected the dining room of their two condos. Using what they called a poor man's intercom, she shouted a warning that she was coming over. She found Steve, not sitting in his recliner, but at the dining room table with laptop and phone at the ready. "You look indus-

32

trious this afternoon," said Heather. "Are you working on your story?"

"That was this morning. I've moved on to current events."

Heather spoke through a yawn. "What's that supposed to mean?"

"Chris and I spoke last night. I'm helping him discover how a foreign substance wound up in the bottle of eye drops."

She interrupted. "I take it the police put a rush on analyzing it?"

Steve gave his head a single nod. "Chris hasn't heard if the damage is permanent. The police came back and took every bottle from Chris's practice."

Heather dug a crusty from the corner of her eye. "That may be enough to put him out of business."

"I asked him that very thing. He's pretty sure nothing that drastic will happen, but he also said if it came down to it, there's enough room on his credit cards to charge what he needs for another month."

Heather groaned. "The interest will eat him alive."

"I offered to make him an interest-free loan, but he turned me down. He believes so much in himself and doing things without help that he's his own worst enemy."

"If Chris is so self-reliant, why did he call you and ask for your help with the eye drops?"

Steve issued an impish smile. "I didn't say he called me, and he certainly didn't ask for my help. I'm a little sensitive to people losing their vision, so this is all my idea."

"What can I do?"

"It's not a murder and there's no client. According to our agreement, those two things have to be present for us to take a case. Besides, you have deals to make and projects to complete, not to mention helping Jack and his mother over this rough spot."

Heather shook her head. "Let me guess. You've already talked to Jack and you know all about Cora's angina."

"You were in no condition to talk when you arrived home this morning."

"I should have known you'd be awake."

"My sleeping schedule doesn't coincide with most people's. It's always night to me."

Heather yawned again. "I feel like a bus ran me over."

"Hospital emergency rooms will do that to you. You were wise to take off today."

Heather slapped her forehead. "Where is my brain? That's why I'm here."

Steve didn't let her finish. "Get a cup of coffee and relax. Jack told me you left your phone charger with him. I wondered if you'd have enough power to call your office this morning, or if you'd even wake up at your normal time. Just in case you slept in, I called your personal assistant and told her you'd be worse than the Wicked Witch of the West if you came in." Steve grinned.

"Seriously, between stress and fatigue, you needed sleep more than pushing yourself to go to work this morning. Your people can handle it for a day."

Heather sighed and rose to pour herself a cup of stimulant. "Well, it's probably not what I would've chosen to do if I hadn't been dead to the world, but thank you for calling for me. It was a long night." She set her coffee cup on the table. "Speaking of phones... Can I borrow your charging cord?"

"Only if you promise not to call your office."

"Now that I know they're not waiting to hear from me, there'll be no work for me today. I'm going to take a ridiculously long bath, find a place where I can get a manicure and pedicure, get the frizzy ends of my hair trimmed, eat a healthy supper, and go to bed early with a good book."

"There's hope for you yet, McBlythe."

"I need to get rested for what lies ahead."

Steve tilted his head. "What do you mean?"

"Call it a woman's intuition. It won't be long before you need my help."

Heather thought she'd outguessed Steve until he said, "There's another reason I called your office and told them you weren't coming in today. If you're not too tired, we'll talk again tonight."

———

HEATHER'S DAY PASSED IN SELF-INDULGENT SLOW MOTION. SHE accomplished all her goals with a couple of modifications. Instead of soaking in a hot tub, she went to the gym, worked on cardio until she achieved a good sweat and followed the workout with time in the sauna to further clear out impurities. She cooled down under a cold shower and replenished lost fluids with a liter of sports drink. Next came a kale, mango, and powdered protein drink from the juice bar. Then came the trip to the beauty salon. Five o'clock traffic caught her on the trip home, after having her nails shaped and leaving the split ends of her auburn hair on the beautician's floor. For once, she didn't mind the slow pace of traffic, and sang along with songs she'd listened to during her freshman year at Princeton.

After throwing her sweaty exercise clothes in the washer, she beat a path next door to see what Steve wanted for supper. It appeared he hadn't moved from the table where she'd left him many hours before.

"Have you been hard at work all day?"

Steve shook his head side to side. "My crazy internal clock told me I needed to take a nap. It lasted four hours, and I missed lunch. I've only been awake long enough to eat your leftover sushi and rice. I hope you don't mind. A replacement order for you is on the way."

"You didn't have to do that, but I'm glad you did."

"If you want something else, I can—"

"Don't even think about it. My stomach growled all last night in the hospital waiting room. I couldn't stop thinking about how good sushi would taste."

Heather changed the subject. "You said earlier you worked on your story this morning. Did that work include some advice from Kate?"

Steve placed his hands over his computer's keyboard. "We talked twice."

His voice came out emotionless. In fact, it came out too flat. Time to back away from what she wanted to ask him and move to something safe. "How's the weather in Miami?"

"Sunny."

"And the temperature?"

"Hot."

"The humidity?"

"Low in her condo. High on the patio overlooking the beach." Steve placed his hands on the table. "I didn't ask about the surf, the tides, the wind speed, the chances of rain, or the pollen count. I also forgot to ask if any major storms were forming off the coast of Africa. We talked about my short story."

Steve took in a breath and let it out in a soft, slow blow. "Sorry. I didn't mean to snap."

Heather patted him on the hand. "No offense taken." She paused. "Well, not much anyway. Some things happened yesterday that have my mind going in different directions. Things between me and Jack."

"Ah. Your relationship is getting serious, and it has you scared."

Heather's head dipped. "You noticed."

"I tested you yesterday by suggesting you buy a sailboat and take it to Belize together. If I'd suggested that a year ago, you'd have laughed and not given it a second thought."

She gave him a pretend punch in the arm. "You old stinker. Is there no end to the mind games you play with people?"

He grinned. "You tried to play the same game with me."

"When?"

"Just now. What difference does it make what the weather is in Miami? You wanted to know if Kate and I are getting serious."

Heather leaned back. "What's the answer?"

Steve rubbed his chin. "I'll give you two answers. The first is, our relationship is where yours was with Jack about a year and a half ago. We live a thousand miles apart and have only been around each other on two occasions."

Heather added, "And both involved us solving murders."

"That brings me to the second answer. You and Jack have very little emotional baggage compared to me and Kate. For me, it's Maggie. I committed until death separated us, which it did. That may be enough for other people to move on, but for me, I'm not sure the marriage contract didn't get an extension."

"But—"

"Let me finish. For Kate, she came out of one of the most abusive marriages anyone can imagine. That creep depleted every bit of trust she had in men. I'll put this as blunt as I can. Kate and I are both damaged goods. We're both scared of making the mistake of following some emotional whim and discovering in a year or two that our past is stronger than the present, or the future."

Steve pushed away from the table, retrieved a glass of water, and sat back down. "In the meantime, Kate and I will continue to focus on stories based on cases I solved when I had my sight."

To add an exclamation mark to the end of talk about relationships, Steve asked, "By the way, how are your mother and father?"

"Good," said Heather before she thought. "Wait. I called Mother from the hall bathroom this morning. That's the one place in my condo those bat ears of yours can't hear what I'm saying. How did you know I called?"

"An educated guess. Cora's trip to the ER had you thinking about the new season of life you and Jack will face, no matter if you do it alone or together. Your parents are reaching the age when things wear out. It made sense you'd want to check on your parents."

The knock on the door saved Heather from telling Steve he'd been a step ahead of her... again.

6

———

Heather admired the new polish on her toenails as she padded her way to Steve's front door. She expected to see the face of the delivery guy bringing a fresh supply of sushi and fried rice, not Detective Hall. He gave her a quick look and said, "Nice color on the nails. That wasn't there yesterday."

She took a step back and swung the door all the way open. "You're more observant than you were when you worked the Ned Logan murder. I notice you don't have Detective Lowe with you."

Hall's next words came out with a sigh. "He doesn't know I'm here, and if it's all the same, I'd like to keep it that way."

"Come in," said Steve. "Don't worry about us giving up your secret. I don't know any good detectives that haven't had to work around something, or someone, in order to solve a case."

Heather closed the door and followed the detective to the dining room. She'd no more sat down when a second knock on the front door caused her to stand. "That has to be my supper."

Sure enough, the same blue-haired delivery driver stood outside with a plastic bag extended and said, "Thanks for the ten-dollar tip you put on your card. It'll sure help get my little girl a new pair of shoes."

Heather reached into the back pocket of her shorts and put her fingers on a ten-dollar bill. "Come in and put the order on the counter." She gave the young man the stare she'd perfected when she interrogated suspects back in Boston. "I'll double your tip if you truthfully answer one question."

The eyes of the delivery driver focused on Heather's forehead. "What's the question?"

She nudged her head toward the dining room. "Before you answer, I need to tell you that a former homicide detective, a police detective, and an attorney will hear your answer. Each of us are experts in determining whether a person is lying or telling the truth. Do you understand?"

"I guess so."

Heather locked her gaze on the man's eyes. "You don't have a daughter, do you?"

He licked his lips before the blue hair swung from side to side. "It's a line my girlfriend made up for me to say to get more tips. She told me to invent multiple stories that would make customers feel sorry for me." He looked down and blew out a breath. "I remember now. I delivered here last night and used the daughter's new shoes story. Sorry."

Heather handed him the ten-dollar bill. "Tell the truth and you'll always get a good tip here. Lie again, and your manager will receive a phone call."

Steve and Detective Hall both muffled a laugh with their hands when Heather returned from the front door. Hall said, "That's what I like about you two—always perfecting your skills. I never would've considered a delivery driver might cook up a scam to get extra tips. How did you know he didn't have a daughter?"

"I didn't, and neither did Steve. The odds were in my favor because of the way I worded the sentence."

Steve added, "Heather turned what could have been a question into an accusation. Young parents are universally proud of their new status and their children. The second the delivery guy hesitated we knew a daughter didn't exist."

Heather popped open the top of a styrofoam container, unwrapped wooden chopsticks, and reached for a packet of soy sauce. "I hope you don't mind if I eat in front of you. My protein shake left me a couple of hours ago."

Steve took over the conversation. "I assume you didn't come here to watch Heather eat or hone your skills of observation and detecting deception in delivery drivers. What's on your mind?"

"Detective Lowe will be back tomorrow after a multi-day vacation. He'll be in a bad mood and will want to sit at his desk, drink coffee, and review the files of the cases I worked. The case in the optometrist's office is the only one I haven't cleared. I'm afraid he'll come in, read the file, and tell me to lean on the ex-wife for a confession. I spoke with her today and she seemed torn up about the injury."

Steve lifted his chin. "Describe how she reacted."

"Like I said, it upset her. She took up for her ex. Said there had to have been tampering at the manufacturer or by someone else. She asked if his practice was open again. When I told her we had to confiscate and check the rest of the medicines for contamination, that really got to her. Said she'd collect what he needed to get him back open."

Heather swallowed a bite of fried rice. "Was she concerned about Chris, or the possibility of not receiving a child support check on time?"

"I may be wrong, but the tears looked real to me. I don't think she'd blubber the way she did over money. Her waiting room was jammed and the retail side of the business had people lined up to try on glasses. I ran a bank check on her and she's sitting flush. I can't say the same for Chris Craddock."

Steve took over again. "Any results from the lab?"

"Not yet. The ophthalmologist that treated Mattie Arnold said Dr. Craddock followed proper medical procedures when he spent so much time irrigating the eye. He doesn't expect permanent damage, but wants the eye to rest a couple of days before checking it again."

Steve summarized. "Chris did everything according to protocol, and his business is deep in debt. His ex-wife can get by fine with a delay in child support, and she seemed abnormally upset about his business having to shut down. She's even sending him supplies so he can reopen as soon as possible. Does that sum up what you saw and heard?"

"That's pretty much it, except I'm afraid Detective Lowe will add two plus two and come up with seven. How can I handle him tomorrow morning?"

Steve puffed out his cheeks and let the air out in a rush. "If it were me, I'd buy time."

"What do you mean?"

"When you need to delay, a bureaucracy, government agency, or a large corporation can be helpful allies. In this case, tell Lowe you think the tampering occurred in the factory. You don't have to be right or even believe it, but it will buy you time while you dig deeper into who has a reason to harm Chris or his practice."

Detective Hall stood. "Thanks. I'll keep digging while my partner eases back into the swing of things."

Steve added another piece of advice. "Dig fast and without noise. You don't have much time. Once the manufacturer goes into a full defense of their reputation, they'll send in investigators and lawyers by the busload. They'll accuse anyone and everyone in order to take the spotlight off themselves. It won't be long before you and Lowe will receive emails and phone calls from your boss wanting this thing to go away."

"Do you think it'll come to that?"

Heather answered for Steve. "As a shark that swims with other attorneys, I can guarantee a drug manufacturer will do what it takes to keep adverse publicity about their product out of the news. It's a safe bet there's a meeting going on right now about who they can blame. The one thing you don't want is your name added to the list."

"Me? Why would they blame me?"

Steve leaned forward. "The press wants a story that goes on and on. The attorneys know this, and they're looking to deflect suspicion from the company that's paying their fat salaries. Until you can give them the person who did this, or their own internal investigation proves otherwise, they'll keep up the narrative of blaming others. If that peters out, they'll accuse the police of incompetence. It's all a smokescreen."

Hall sat down again and rubbed his temples. "How did this simple case get so complicated?"

Steve shifted to face Heather. "I know this isn't in our contract, but are you well rested?"

"I slept until noon today."

"Good." Steve turned to face Detective Hall. "What about you? Are you ready for a late night of doing background checks?"

"Huh?"

Heather rose and moved toward the coffeepot. "Steve and I need the names of all the employees who work for Chris Craddock and his ex-wife. Also, any employees who've worked for either of them in the last six months."

Steve corrected her. "Make that the last twelve months."

Heather continued. "If all three of us work on this, we'll have a good start on suspects. That should give you plenty to get ahead of the vultures before they swoop down."

Steve added, "It will also show your supervisors you haven't been sitting on your hands. Lowe will probably take credit for all the work we'll do tonight, but that's the way it goes."

Heather looked down at her food. "I can't be eating alone. Who wants pizza?"

Steve held up a hand. "You can't start a thorough investigation without pizza."

Hall also raised his hand. "Pizza's good, but I'd rather have a partner like either of you."

"Remember that when you're promoted to senior partner,"

said Steve. "You can help mold your partner into something special."

Hall stood again. "I need to run out to my car and grab my computer."

After Hall closed the door, Heather scooped Honduran coffee into a paper filter. "He's a good cop."

Steve countered with, "Still a little green, but he has what it takes."

Talk ceased as Heather filled the reservoir with water and punched the buttons required to bring the brewer to life. She leaned against the counter. "What bothers you most about this case?"

"Motive." He hesitated, then continued. "We both know that at least ninety-nine percent of what we'll do tonight is wasted effort, but it has to be done. I've been rolling around what happened to Mattie Arnold in my mind since yesterday, at least when I wasn't sleeping. The only thing I can come up with for a motive is that someone wants Chris to fail, and fail big. Why? That's what has me stumped."

Heather took her phone off the table and punched in a number she'd called many times before. "Do you want the standard order?"

"Yeah. Meat lover's supreme with extra cheese."

"Anything else?"

"A side order of the person who hurt an innocent college girl."

Heather tucked a lock of hair behind her ear. "If it were only that easy." She finished placing the order as Hall reentered the condo. "You're getting a meat lover's supreme with extra cheese. I hope that's all right with you."

"Perfect. Let me get the tip when the delivery guy arrives."

Steve chuckled. "It'll give you a chance to practice recognizing deception."

7

Heather listened as the pizza guy handed the cardboard package to Detective Hall and received a ten-dollar tip. Hall asked, "Any kids at home?"

A look of confusion passed over the face of the driver. He shrugged and said, "*No entiendo Inglés. Gracias por el propina.*" The man spun on the heel of his tennis shoes and was gone before Heather could control her chuckle.

Hall shook his head. "Why did I take French in high school and college?"

Heather took the box from him. "He said he doesn't understand English and thanks for the tip."

Steve spoke from his chair in the dining room. "A course in conversational Spanish would be a plus for your career."

"That's not a bad idea if I stay with the P.D."

Heather glanced at Steve to see if he wanted to pursue this discussion or wanted her to. She had her answer when Steve asked, "Are you shopping for something different?"

"Sit down," said Heather. "I'll get plates and something besides coffee to wash down the pizza."

Hall settled himself again in front of his laptop and folded down the screen. "Up to now, all I've done is talk to people in

45

other agencies—local, state, and federal. My partner lost interest in his job a long time ago. It's like I'm stuck in the only lane of the freeway that isn't moving."

Steve pushed his laptop to the center of the table, making way for Heather to deliver the first two slices of pizza. Instead of diving in, he restrained himself long enough to ask, "Do you think moving to another agency will get you back into the fast lane?"

"Some people I've talked to told me getting a fresh start was the best decision they ever made, and others said the opposite. To tell you the truth, I don't know what to think."

"Is the problem the job or your partner?"

Heather thought about asking the same question. Based on what Hall had said, and her and Steve's prior experience with Detective Lowe, she believed a new partner might cure what ailed the bright young detective.

"It seems I'm stuck with him. I went to my lieutenant and asked for a different partner, but she told me I needed to stick it out. Gave me that tired old line of putting in my dues and overcoming adversity."

The conversation hit a lull while the two men polished off their first two pieces. Heather placed two more smaller pieces in front of Steve. He picked up a slice and held it up as he spoke. "The problem with asking others about such an important decision is, most people are too willing to give advice. They can tell you what they think they would do, but they aren't you and it won't affect them. You're the only one who has to live with the decision."

Heather joined in the conversation. "Tell him how you almost left the force when Houston P.D. had you working stolen cars."

Steve put the slice of pizza back on his plate. "It was the most dead-end job you can imagine. I thought if I recovered the most cars, the department would reward my initiative and it would help me fast-track into Homicide. Talk about making a bad assumption. The captain over stolen vehicles gave me all kinds of meaningless certificates that he made up. None of them ended up in my personnel file. It took me two years to realize all he cared about was the overall numbers of recovered vehicles. You think you're in the slow lane? My lane didn't move at all, and it wasn't going to."

"What did you do?"

"Heather, you tell him. I don't like cold pizza."

She rolled her eyes. "He did a work-around on a homicide case that was none of his business. A crusty old detective took pity on him and gave him the chance to work on a tricky murder."

Steve spoke around a bite of pizza. "It was my make-or-break moment. If I didn't make detective in Homicide, I was turning in my badge. It was solving murders or selling insurance."

Hall tilted his head. "You're joking. You must have been seven or eight years into your career."

"And I would have started all over again doing something else." Steve reached for his glass of iced tea. "That was the decision I made. Your story is different, but similar. Only you can decide what's best for you."

Heather sat down. "While you two stuff your faces, I'm doing a credit check on Sandi Fields. Let's see if she pays her bills on time."

Hall pursed his lips. "Is everything you two do legal?"

Heather looked at Steve and burst out laughing, so he was the first to answer. "When was the last time you heard of a rich attorney getting arrested for doing something to help with a police investigation?"

Heather reached out and placed a hand on Hall's forearm. "I watched you type in your password to The Woodlands P.D. database. I won't get in trouble for this."

Steve added, "That's what I meant by finding a work-around. There are other ways she could do the credit check, but using your password was the fastest. By the way, she sent me a text message with your sign in and password. I have access too."

"Did you run a credit check on me while I answered the door for the delivery guy?"

Steve brushed away the question with a wave of his hand. "Of course not, but I ran one on your partner. Did you know he bought a new truck last week?"

Hall put his hands over his ears. "I didn't hear that."

Steve issued a single clap of his hands. "Now you're catching on. Selective hearing is another thing a good detective needs to develop."

Evening turned into night, which gave way to the wee hours of the morning. Heather stifled a yawn as Detective Hall left at 1:37 a.m. He took with him emails containing background information and the criminal histories of Chris Craddock's employees and those of his ex-wife.

Max waited for Heather on the pillow beside hers. She spent a few minutes reviewing the day and how much she enjoyed sleeping late, missing work, and especially taking the time to pamper herself. She fell asleep wondering why she didn't do it more often.

The next morning, she was up, dressed, and ready to face another day at her office when she heard Steve's phone ringing. His muffled voice didn't allow her to hear his words. She was about to shout at him through Max's special door when the flap opened.

"Detective Hall called. There's a body in Melody Craddock's eyeglass store."

Heather stood in stunned silence for several seconds. She placed her work valise on the dining room table, bent down to the kitty door, and pushed open the flap. "I'm coming over."

Steve looked as though he'd slept with his head in a vice. The top resembled the long grass that borders driveways and sidewalks, while the sides lay flat. "Did Hall give you any details?"

"Only that Detective Lowe called in sick today."

Heather issued a scoffing laugh, then gave a tepid apology. "Sorry. It's possible he's really sick."

"It's more likely he came down with a case of back-to-work-itis." Steve squared his shoulders. "Enough chit-chat. Hall wants us to come to Melody's clinic and for you to look at the scene before they move the body."

"You're not going anywhere until you shower, shave, and do something with that porcupine hairdo."

Steve's phone came to life again. It announced the caller's name, and he put it on speaker. "Good morning, Chris."

A voice laced with panic came through the speaker. "Have you heard about Melody's store? Someone's out to get both of us."

Steve countered with a calm response. "Take a deep breath. I've already spoken with the detective in charge of the case. There's a lot we don't know yet. Heather's on her way to Melody's office, and I need to hop in the shower. The only thing you're to do is drive over and pick me up."

Chris acted like he couldn't take everything in. "I need to get to Melody." He took in a sharp breath. "Tell me what you know."

"Only that they found the night cleaning woman unresponsive when the staff arrived this morning."

"Melody needs me. I'm going there now."

"Not without me. The cops won't treat Melody the same way they did you yesterday. They'll separate her from everyone and question her. The only exception will be if Heather tells them she's Melody's attorney. I know you think getting to Melody as fast as you can will help, but it won't."

"There has to be something more I can do."

"Call Jack and see if he can meet us at Melody's. I don't mean to frighten you, but for the time being, you need to play defense, and that includes having an attorney to make sure you don't say or do anything you'll be sorry for later."

"What about Melody?"

"That's why Heather's on her way."

"I don't care what this costs me. I don't want Melody's reputation dragged through the mud."

Steve motioned for Heather to leave and continued to talk to Chris. "Before I hang up, tell me the two things you're going to do."

"Call Jack and come get you."

"That's all you need to concentrate on for now."

With the call disconnected and her hand on the doorknob, Heather turned her head to Steve. "Does this mean he hired us?"

"Not yet. All we know is there's a dead cleaning lady at Melody Craddock's retail store."

"You don't fool me, Steve. You sensed something was going to happen or you wouldn't have kept us up last night doing preliminary work."

He waved as he walked away.

8

An officer stopped Heather at the police tape. She showed him her credentials identifying her as an attorney, and asked him to notify Detective Hall of her arrival. He complied, but with a look of distrust. A few seconds later, Hall strode across the front parking spots of the strip mall and announced, "Let her pass."

Heather ducked under the yellow tape and put on gloves and booties offered by the detective.

Hall said, "You know the drill. Look but don't touch."

Heather nodded. "I know it well. Where is she?"

"By the center work station."

Hall led the way. Posters near the door screamed *SALE*. The two side walls and part of the back wall bristled with racks of eyeglasses and vanity mirrors. Posters of pretty people wearing designer eyeglasses formed a border above and between the displays. Each of the posed models smiled like they enjoyed wearing extra weight on their face. A half-dozen tables, each with a computer screen, keyboard, sales brochures, and a mirror on a stand, dotted the sales floor. A credit card reader stood at the ready beside the computer keyboards. The center section of the sales area held a twenty-by-twenty work station that included short file cabinets and trays of glasses.

Hall walked around the center section, whose walls rose to about four and a half feet. He pointed down at a lifeless body. "The victim is Cleopatra Elizabeth Stanley, forty-six-years old, lives in Conroe. Everyone I talked to knew her as Cleo."

Heather looked down at the woman, whose left temple had a slight cut. Curly silver hair contrasted with her ebony skin.

"Not much blood." Heather looked at the sharp corner of the workstation and pointed. "There's some on this corner."

"Yeah. I noticed it. What do you make of the vacuum cleaner by her? It was still running when the first worker arrived."

Heather took a close look at a pair of headphones near Cleo's head. "Those are noise cancelling. She may not have heard a thing." She took a longer look around the room and returned her gaze to Hall. "As far as crime scenes go, this is one of the cleanest. Do you think she might have gotten dizzy and fallen while cleaning?"

"I did at first. Follow me."

The back wall had a door opening to a hallway. Off the hall sat a workroom, a small office with the door open, and a break room. "Take a look," said Hall when he reached the office with its door open.

Heather stood at the doorway, but didn't go in. A black metal file cabinet stood on the other side of a utilitarian desk with its second drawer halfway open. A couple of files and scattered papers littered the floor.

Heather nodded. "That changes everything."

"Yeah. It looks like a burglary gone bad."

"Is there a back door?"

Hall nodded. "Still locked, and secured with a bar."

"Have you checked to see if any ceiling tiles are disturbed?"

"Not yet, but it's on my list."

"Any keys missing?"

"Also on my list. I'll let you know later."

Heather turned to leave and Hall followed. They went back to where Cleo Stanley lay. "Who found the body?"

"A man named Bryson Wayne. He's the sales manager here on the retail side. Arrived a couple of minutes before seven. Says he came in early to process paperwork and put out a shipment of new frames. He found her, turned off the vacuum cleaner, and called 911 from his cell phone."

"What do you make of him?"

"He wears skinny jeans, loafers without socks, and may still be crying. At first glance, he's an unlikely suspect. He's next door in the optometry office waiting room."

Hall pointed down at Cleo. "What are your first impressions?"

Heather took in a deep breath. "Steve always cautions about forming conclusions too soon, but from what I see, there are two possibilities. The first is, someone broke into the building, stole something out of the file cabinet in the back, and left before Cleo started cleaning. That would make it possible for her death to be an accident."

"What about the fact that the vacuum's cord is wrapped around her ankles?"

Heather took another look. "It could have caused her to fall." She took a breath. "Or, it happened when someone pushed her."

"And that's the second possibility? Someone pushed her?"

"Here's how it could have happened. Cleo came in and started cleaning the showroom. This surprised the burglar, causing him or her to scatter files. They panicked, made a run for the front door, and shoved Cleo on their way out. Her head struck the sharp corner, and she never woke up." Heather took a breath. "Of course, Steve will come up with a half-dozen other scenarios for how it happened."

Hall squatted and looked at Cleo. "I don't like the coincidence that the other day a routine eye exam went wrong and today I'm looking at a dead woman. The two optometrists that own both businesses share the last name of Craddock."

Heather asked, "Have you spoken with Melody Craddock yet?"

"She should arrive any minute."

"Steve and Chris Craddock are on their way, too. My boyfriend, Jack Blackstock, might show up."

"The attorney?"

"Yeah. Do you know him?"

"He ripped me apart on the witness stand last year." He glanced at Heather and smiled as they walked to the front door. "Let's call it a learning experience for me."

They walked out the front door and took a hard right. The next door they came to had Melody's name, title, and office hours on it. Detective Hall stopped in front of the door and looked down at Heather from his height of six foot, two inches. "I need to ask you something. Are you and Jack Blackstock here to represent Chris and Melody Craddock?"

"Steve spoke with Chris this morning, and he wants to make sure we protect Melody in every way possible. That could be Jack's job, if he takes it. So, the answer is no concerning me being Chris or Melody's attorney. After what Chris did to save Mattie Arnold's sight, I'm not sure he needs an attorney. Steve and I will focus on helping you find the truth behind this death and what happened to Mattie Arnold."

Hall's attention shifted to the parking lot beyond the police tape. A woman approached with concern etched on her face. Her clothes, makeup, and hair all spoke of a thirty-something, attractive, professional woman. She said a few words to the officer, and he raised the tape for her.

Hall took a couple of steps toward the woman. "Dr. Craddock?"

"Yes."

"I'm Detective Hall with The Woodlands Police Department." He turned his shoulders. "This is Heather McBlythe. It's my understanding your former husband—"

"Chris called me and told me Ms. McBlythe would be here."

She turned to face Heather. "I feel like I've known you for a long time, even though we've never met. Jack was gob-struck the first time he met you. Now I see why."

"That's very kind."

Detective Hall opened the door of the optometry office. "Ms. McBlythe tells me Mr. Blackstock may be on his way."

"He called while I drove here and told me to hold off answering questions until he arrives."

"I expected that. Ms. McBlythe and I will speak to your sales clerk, Bryson Wayne. He found Mrs. Stanley when he opened this morning."

"Can you tell me what happened?"

Heather broke in. "Departmental policy prohibits Detective Hall from discussing details at this time. But that doesn't mean I can't. One of your employees found the body of a woman believed to be your night cleaning worker. The cause of death won't be determined until later."

Melody shook her head. "Poor Cleo. She leaves behind a diabetic husband, six children, and Lord knows how many grand-children."

An awkward silence fell on the reception area.

"Perhaps," said Heather, "my business partner, Steve Smiley, and I could take you for coffee after you and Jack speak with Detective Hall."

Melody looked at the rows of empty chairs. "I suppose this means I'll need to cancel all appointments today."

Hall looked at his watch. "I'd like you available to answer questions this morning, but I see no reason you shouldn't keep afternoon appointments. The retail shop is a different story. Crime scene technicians are very methodical and messy, especially with fingerprint powder. I suggest you call a cleaning service and have them on standby."

The front door flew open and in walked Chris, Jack, and Steve. After giving Jack a quick wink, Heather focused on Chris as he took long strides toward Melody. He greeted her with a full hug, but her hands stayed at her side.

"Are you all right, Mel?"

She took a step back. "I'm stunned, but fine otherwise."

"Don't worry. Everything's going to be fine. We'll get through this." He glanced at Jack and then brought his gaze back to his ex-wife. "I brought Jack. He'll guide you. Be sure to do everything he says."

Melody straightened her posture. "That's good advice. I hope you did the same."

Heather saw Chris's shoulders stiffen, but he gave no other indicator of offense.

Detective Hall interrupted. "To avoid confusion, I'm going to call Dr. Melody Craddock, Dr. Melody. Dr. Chris Craddock will be Dr. Chris."

"Good idea," said Jack. "I need a private office to converse with Dr. Melody."

"I want to tag along," said Dr. Chris.

"Sorry," said Jack. "All discussions between me and Melody are confidential."

"But..." Chris bit off his objection. "Oh, all right."

Detective Hall cast his gaze to Chris. "While Mr. Blackstock and Dr. Melody are talking, I need to ask you a few questions, Dr. Chris."

"Me? I thought we already talked about everything. Jack told me not to say anything if he wasn't present."

Heather didn't give Chris a chance to reply any further. "Steve and I can start with Bryson Wayne, if that's all right with you, Detective."

"I'm through with him for now. You'll find Mr. Wayne in Dr. Melody's office."

Heather placed Steve's hand on her forearm and followed Dr. Melody, Jack, and Detective Hall through a doorway that led to the examination rooms and other offices. Dr. Melody stopped at a closed door. "This is my office."

Hall knocked on the door and pushed it open. The man at the desk had a cell phone to his ear as he spun around to face the group.

"Got to dash. I'll call back when I hear when we'll be open again."

Detective Hall motioned for Heather and Steve to enter. "Mr. Wayne, this is Heather McBlythe and Steve Smiley. They're assisting me with the investigation. I'd appreciate it if you'd cooperate with them as fully as you did with me."

The man rose and looked past them to Dr. Melody. "I called my sales team and told them not to even drive by until you gave the all clear. Detective Hall said it could be a day or two before we can reopen."

Melody took a step into her office. "When you get a chance, find a company that specializes in cleaning crime scenes. Tell them what happened and that you'll need a rush job done as soon as we can reopen. I don't want you or your crew missing any more work than necessary."

"Consider it done."

Detective Hall announced, "I'm going back to the lobby and speak with Dr. Chris."

Melody turned to Jack. "There are plenty of rooms for a quiet conversation. Let's go find one and you can coach me on what not to say."

The door closed and Bryson Wayne moved away from the desk and executive chair. "Here, Ms. McBlythe. This one's nice and comfy."

"I'll put Steve there. You know what they say about age before beauty."

Bryson let out a high-pitched giggle. He pulled out a chair for Heather and soon had a triangle formed at the perfect distance to converse but not feel crowded. "I should apologize for laughing."

"Not at all," said Steve. "It's one of the coping mechanisms people use in stressful situations. I've witnessed it hundreds of times."

Heather explained. "Steve was a homicide detective in Houston for many years, until he lost his sight."

Bryson crossed skinny legs into a tight twist. His right foot dangled loose, almost touching the ground. "And what about you, Ms. McBlythe? Secret Service? CIA? Didn't you have a role in the last Bond film?"

It was Heather's turn to laugh. "Hardly. I'm an attorney and a former cop in Boston."

He wagged an index finger. "I thought I detected an accent."

Steve broke in. "Tell us about finding the body this morning."

Bryson held out a hand and let it drop at the wrist, as if it were too heavy to hold out straight. "Oh, my goodness. It was the most gosh-awful thing that ever happened to me. I've never seen a dead person before." He paused. "I take that back. They encouraged everyone to view the deceased at the funeral of a friend. I almost fainted."

"Did you use your keys to open the door?"

He looked at the ceiling. "Yes. I'm positive I did."

Heather made a mental note to ask Detective Hall if Cleo Stanley had keys to the business on her or in her purse.

Steve pressed on. "Start with you opening the door and tell us everything you did, saw, heard, or smelled. Don't leave anything out. Close your eyes if that helps you remember."

Following Steve's suggestion, Bryson squeezed his eyelids shut. "I'm turning the key clockwise in the lock. I returned the keys to the right front pocket of my pants. All the lights are on as I walk in."

"Is that unusual?"

Bryson opened his eyes. "Yes, and no. The first thing I do every morning is turn on all the lights. I didn't need to this morning, because I arrived so early."

"Keep going," said Steve.

Bryson closed his eyes again. "I heard the vacuum cleaner running, so I went to say hello to Cleo."

"Did you touch anything on the way?"

"No. I always walk fast, and I didn't stop until I noticed Cleo's feet sticking out from behind the back of the counter in the center of the room."

"Did you touch the body?"

"Heavens, no. I called to her, but of course she didn't answer."

Steve said, "Stop for a moment and look at Cleo. Are any of her clothes torn or out of place?"

"No. At first, I thought she might have passed out or might have nodded off."

"Look around. Do you notice anything out of place?"

"Everything is as it should be. I make it a point to look at the displays of glasses as I come in. It's my way of taking a quick inventory. There were no gaps, which means the evening crew restocked before they left last night."

"Did you go into the work area in the center of the store?"

Bryson shook his head. "I'm not into hanging around people who aren't moving or breathing. I ran to the front door, called 911, and waited in the parking lot for police and EMS to arrive."

"Did you notice anything suspicious in the parking lot?"

"At that hour, my car and one other were the only ones there. When I told Detective Hall about it, he said the other car belonged to Cleo."

"You didn't know Cleo?"

Bryson opened his eyes again. "I knew we had a night cleaner, and I knew her name, but that's all."

Steve thanked Bryson and told him to check with Detective Hall about what to do next.

Once Heather and Steve were in the office alone with the door shut, Steve pulled off his sunglasses and rubbed his sightless eyes. "That wasn't much help."

"We've started with less," said Heather.

As they stepped into the hall, Jack and Melody rounded the

corner leading from the bank of examination rooms. Jack spoke first. "Are you through with Melody's office?"

"We're finished with Bryson Wayne."

"Go back in and I'll get Detective Hall."

"With or without Chris?" asked Steve.

"Without," said Melody, with more emphasis than necessary.

Heather thought back to a conversation with Jack where he'd told her about Chris and Melody's divorce. She'd need to press him harder for details. Something about Chris didn't sit right, which wasn't unusual for her. After law school and ten years of being a cop, her trust in humanity, and divorced men in particular, wasn't high.

As soon as the door clicked shut behind her, Melody addressed Steve and Heather. "I don't know what Chris has told you about our divorce, but don't believe him."

9

Dr. Melody opened the door again to her office and returned to her chair. Jack and Detective Hall entered. Melody said, "Jack, you can bring in another chair from the office next door."

Detective Hall held up his hand to stop Jack. "Don't worry about me not having a place to sit. The forensic team is here and I need to make this quick." His gaze focused on Melody. "Can you account for your whereabouts last night?"

"All night?"

"From ten o'clock until this morning when Bryson Wayne arrived at work."

Melody looked at Jack, who gave her a nod of his head, showing she could answer. Her shoulders dropped a fraction. "That's easy. I was home with my children. They're seven and four, so I never leave them unattended."

Jack spoke up. "Melody has a motion-activated security system that records audio and video of any unusual activity. I'll get you the contact information of the firm that monitors it."

"That would be helpful. Thanks."

Hall looked at all the occupants of the room, one by one. "I have a list of questions I'll need answers to. This may be unorthodox, but I'd like you four to go somewhere and get a cup of coffee. If Steve and Heather come back with answers to the questions I need to ask, it will save me a great deal of time. I appreciate your cooperation."

Jack spoke up. "I can't guarantee they'll have answers to all the questions you need to ask."

Hall nodded. "I'll take what I can get for now. My senior partner's coming back today, and the more answers I have when he returns, the happier we'll all be."

Jack looked at his watch. "I understand."

Hall cast a hard gaze at Jack until he made eye contact. "I also understand that at the first sign of undue pressure, you'll advise your client to say nothing without you being present."

Jack nodded. An agreement formed between the two men that involved everyone in the room. Steve and Heather would get information from Melody. Jack would review it to make sure nothing threw suspicion her way. Finally, if they took care of things today, they could avoid wasting time with a hard-nosed cop used to doing things his way.

Heather lifted her chin. "That website we worked on last night. Are all the forms we need on it?"

Hall nodded. "Everything is there but my signature."

Steve cleared his throat. "I don't know about the rest of you, but I could use coffee and a blueberry muffin."

Hall turned to leave as Melody stood and said, "I know the perfect place. Two blocks down on the right. The early morning crowd should be gone by now."

Once outside and past the police tape, Melody suggested they all go in one vehicle, as the coffee shop had limited parking. They came to Heather's two-month-old Mercedes SUV first, so they pressed it into service as the group's taxi.

"Nice ride," said Melody, as Heather left the parking lot. "My kids will soon outgrow our sedan and I can't decide between the Mercedes and the Lexus."

"Those were my two top choices," said Heather. "I believe you'd be happy with either."

Jack spoke from the back seat. "Heather's a little pickier than me. As long as I have something to haul a boat in the summer and a camper trailer to the deer lease in the winter, I'm happy."

Steve turned to face Jack. "Heather told me you're thinking about getting something electric."

"That's for around town, but I hate to get rid of the Camaro."

Heather looked in her rearview mirror. "He's holding on with both hands to his passing youth." At that moment, she looked at her hands on the steering wheel. The first vestiges of blue veins peeked through the skin. At first, she wrote it off to not being in the sun long enough to get a tan. Then the truth hit her. Somehow, she'd soon slide down the far side of thirty and would, in a few short years, hit the milestone used to separate young from old—forty.

"How much farther?" asked Heather to keep from thinking about her imagined status as a spinster.

"Half a block, on the right."

Though locally owned, the coffee shop patterned itself after the upscale places with an emphasis on baristas in their twenties, foreign names for the cup sizes, and coffees with enough shots of caffeine to make a sloth scale the sheer face of a glacier.

Everyone placed their order without a problem until it was Steve's turn. "I need a cup of coffee."

"What size?" asked the young woman with a pierced lip.

"Whatever fits in a mug."

"We offer *estándar, grandé,* and *muy grandé,* unless you want *disparó* simple or *disparó* double."

"Huh?"

Heather came to Steve's rescue. "Give him a grandé Americana, no room."

Steve faced the server. "Yeah. Whatever she said. Do you have blueberry muffins?"

Once again, Heather spoke for Steve. "He'll take the *pastelería con frambuesas.*"

On the way to their seats, Steve said, "When did we have to leave America to get a cup of coffee and something sweet?"

Heather shook her head. "You're getting a medium-size cup of black coffee and a pastry with raspberry filling."

Steve thought for a minute. "The only reason they use a foreign language is so they can charge more."

Melody joined them and settled in the last bar-height chair.

Steve felt the top of the table. "Isn't this a little small?"

Heather patted his arm. "It's intended to be small. More of an international vibe where people sit close together."

"Ah. Is there anyone near us?"

"No. We're way in the back."

"Is that woman bringing us our order?"

"She'll call us when it's ready."

Jack chuckled. Heather gave him a sideways look and brought her gaze to Melody. "Don't let Steve fool you. It's a game he plays and Jack's not above egging him on. They believe places like this gouge the customers so they pretend not to know how to order."

"They do gouge," said Jack and Steve together.

Steve carried on. "My coffee cost twice as much as coffee at Denny's, and they bring a full carafe to the table."

Heather folded her arms. "Like I said, a silly game played by a couple of overgrown boys."

Melody showed her first smile of the day. "If you're trying to get my mind off what happened today, it's working. Thanks."

Steve leaned toward Heather, but spoke loud enough for everyone at the table to hear. "She's caught on to our plan. Soften her up with humor, then grill her with bright lights and the leading questions."

Jack added, "Bring on the rubber hoses and waterboard. My client has nothing to hide."

"I believe you," said Steve in a more serious tone. "We

already know you didn't leave your house last night. Heather hasn't had a chance yet to tell me what she learned when she arrived and examined the crime scene."

The employee with the pierced lip shouted out Heather's name. Jack rose. "Keep your seats while I get the orders. I'll expect a tip for playing the role of waitress."

"They're called servers these days," said Heather in a correcting voice.

"Don't forget napkins," said Steve.

While Jack went to retrieve coffee and pastries for four, Steve spoke to Melody. "We may joke from time to time, but believe me when I say we take homicides seriously."

Heather added, "Steve has good reason to."

Melody's chin went to her chest. "I remember Jack telling Chris how your wife died, and you lost your sight. That happened my second year at the University of Houston College of Optometry. I'm so sorry."

Steve nodded, but said nothing for a few seconds. "I guess that would stick in the mind of a future optometrist."

"Our professor spoke with your ophthalmologist and explained to us why your injury can't be corrected."

Steve squared his shoulders. "Most doctors I've seen add something to what you just said."

"What's that?"

"They say something like, 'Your injury can't be corrected with today's technology, but significant advancements are being made every day.'"

Melody kept her gaze locked on Steve. "I think it's cruel to give patients false hope. If advancements take place, I'll embrace them. Until then, I treat what's in front of me with available tools and techniques."

Jack delivered the orders, and everyone took a sip of their coffee. Steve broke the quiet. "Heather, you're falling down on your job. You didn't ask them to cut up my pastry. If I pick this up and try to eat it, I'll wear half of it out of here."

"I'll do it," said Melody. "I'm used to doing this for my kids."

"Thanks," said Steve. "Heather, we need you to tell us what you saw at the crime scene this morning."

Normally Steve wouldn't have her give a report in front of a suspect. This was his way of telling her he'd eliminated Melody from that list.

Jack took a notebook and pen from the pocket of his jacket.

Heather gave a step-by-step account starting with the mistrust of the first officer she met, whose name tag read Oliver, to the time she left the building.

"Wow," said Melody. "That's detailed."

By the time Heather finished, Steve had polished off his pastry and done so without a single red drip on his shirt. He lowered his paper cup of coffee. "Give me more detail on the files scattered on the floor of the office in the back of the building."

"Two standard manila files with white tabs. I couldn't get close enough to read anything."

Melody spoke without being prompted. "If they came out of the second drawer, that's the file cabinet holding all the financial records."

Steve gave Heather a break from speaking. "Who has access to those files?"

"All eight of the sales staff put in data on the computer, but only two have access to the complete financial records of the retail store. I'm trying to go green and do away with as much paper as possible. Still, there are tax returns and other documents we have to keep hard copies of. As far as who has access, there's Bryson, the sales manager and Cindy Green, the senior salesperson on the evening shift. Of course, there's me."

Steve took in a deep breath. "What about Chris? Did he keep a key to the buildings or the file cabinets?"

"I hired a top-notch attorney when I decided to divorce him. She guided me into protecting all the assets of the company, as well as my personal ones. Until the divorce became final, a neutral third-party CPA controlled the finances. Neither of us had access to company records until everything was final. As for the keys, he said he lost them. Eventually, I got them back, but I wouldn't put it past him to have made another set."

"You don't believe either Bryson or Cindy Green would have given Chris keys to the showroom or file cabinet after the divorce?"

The answer came back swift and sure. "No way. You've met Bryson, so you have a good idea of his attitude toward violence. As for Cindy, she was one of the employees Chris tried to get touchy-feely with."

Steve brought his paper cup with the plastic lid back to his lips, Heather's cue to ask the next question. "You said you have eight employees working on the retail side. Do any of them stand out in any way?"

"How do you mean?"

"Any disciplinary problems? Do any of them hound you for a pay raise? Malcontents?"

"Nothing like that. They're all on salary plus commission, and I make sure they can earn significant bonuses for achieving sales goals. Of course, some are more successful than others, but they know they're bringing home more than they can earn at other stores." She used her forefinger to outline the lid of her cup. "Believe it or not, Bryson is an excellent interviewer for new employees. He weeds out those who don't have what it takes to be productive."

Jack picked up his cup as he stood. "If you'll excuse me, I have another appointment in a few minutes. I'll leave you in excellent hands, Melody. Call if you have questions."

Jack ran his hand over Heather's shoulders as he left.

Steve stood and unfurled his cane. "Jack forgot he didn't bring his car."

Heather looked up as Jack reentered the coffee shop, shaking his head as he walked to their table.

"Forget something?" asked Steve.

"I couldn't stand to be away from Heather for another second."

Melody let out a groan. "Don't believe him."

"That reminds me," said Heather. "I need to fill out a report for Hall about this interview."

"Take me away from this high-priced place," said Steve. "We need to pump Detective Hall for more information while we still can."

10

A s Heather turned into the parking lot of Melody's office, Jack let out a low whistle. "Someone spent a wad of money on that new truck."

"What is it?" asked Steve.

"A brand-spanking-new Dodge Ram 3500 dually, with the 6.7 liter Cummings turbo-diesel engine. It's silver, with all the bells and whistles."

Heather glanced in the rearview mirror. "You said you're satisfied with your old truck."

"I didn't say I wanted to buy it, just admiring."

Melody kept her gaze on her office. "That's what Chris told me before he brought home a Porsche Boxer so he could look cool driving a two-seater sports car. We had one child in preschool and another in diapers."

Heather parked next to Jack's Camaro. "Back to work for both of us."

He nodded. "I'll call you tonight."

"See that you do."

He gave her a wolfish smile. "Should I come over and get a first-hand account of how your day went?"

"I like the sound of it, but I'll probably be catching up on whatever I'm missing at the office today."

He shrugged. "Suit yourself. I think I'll hit a bucket of balls at the driving range instead." He pointed at Melody as she waited for Heather and Steve to join her at the front of Heather's vehicle. "Can you keep an eye on her today? I'm in court most of the afternoon."

"Sure. Go earn a living."

Jack cleared the parking lot before Heather, Steve, and Melody made it inside. Detective Hall rushed to meet them as they entered Melody's practice. Lines of worry creased his forehead. "I'm glad you're back. Can we go someplace private?"

Melody led the way through the waiting room, into her office, and shut the door.

"What's wrong?" asked Heather.

Hall ran his hand down his face. "Detective Lowe showed up about ten minutes ago. Somehow, our captain found out he skipped work yesterday."

Steve asked, "Is that his new truck in the parking lot?"

Hall gave his head an exaggerated nod. "He may not be so fond of it right now. It seems he spent all day yesterday at the dealership having it worked on."

Heather said, "I don't suppose he's in the best of moods."

"That's an understatement. He hasn't stopped barking since he arrived. He bawled me out for allowing Dr. Melody to go get a cup of coffee."

Steve used his cane to find a seat and settled in. "If he comes looking for Melody, he'll want to know why we're here."

"What should I say?"

"When all else fails, tell the truth." He paused. "Or at least part of the truth."

"What are you up to?" asked Heather.

"You didn't get your eyes examined like you were supposed to yesterday." He turned from her. "Melody, can you give Heather an eye exam?"

"Sure. Since I had to cancel all my morning patients, my calendar is open."

Heather's heart began to jump rope. "Hold on a minute. I can't... I can't have my eyes dilated. I have to drive us home."

Melody brushed away the argument. "Considering the circumstances, I won't dilate. In fact, I'll do a refraction, take a peek at what's going on inside your eyes, and make recommendations for a follow up if I find anything."

Steve didn't allow Heather to come up with another excuse. "Jack says she's having a hard time reading fine print and I've noticed her complaining about headaches. Can you two do that now while I give Detective Hall a quick rundown of what we discussed over coffee?"

"We have our choice of exam rooms," said Melody. "Everything I need is there."

The hallway leading to the exam room looked a mile long to Heather. Once there, the alien-looking instruments used to test eyes caused her to stop in the doorway. Melody's hand rested on her shoulder. "I know you're frightened, but there's nothing to worry about."

After a full breath and a slow release, Heather closed her eyes, took four steps forward, and heard the door click shut behind her. Then came Melody's reassuring voice. "Let me move this monster out of the way for now." She pushed aside a machine straight out of a steam-punk novel and motioned with her hand for Heather to sit in what looked like an uncomfortable chair. "I won't leave you. All we're going to do for the next few minutes is set up your chart."

"While you do that, I need to write a report." Heather drew her laptop out of a valise. "Don't worry, I'm used to answering questions while I work."

Melody took her time, asked all the standard demographic questions, typed answers on the keyboard, and cracked a few jokes. Heather didn't tighten up again until Melody asked about medical history.

Looking over the screen of her computer, she said, "That may be why I'm acting so foolish. I'm in perfect health and always have been. No broken bones, no childhood diseases, not even a runny nose when I watch a sappy movie about someone dying."

"What about dogs or cats dying?" asked Melody, with a gleam of mirth in her eye.

"That's a different story. I can't imagine what a wreck I'll be when Max goes."

"Dog or cat?"

"Maine Coon cat. He's huge, spoiled, and adorable. Sleeps on the pillow next to me. Steve lives next door and we share him."

"I'd love to meet him." She turned from the computer screen. "Okay. I believe we're ready to get started, and I promise to take everything slow."

Heather's features tightened. She closed her laptop and placed it on an empty chair.

Melody reached for what looked like a plastic eye patch attached to a black handle. She then turned off the overhead light. "You're going to see some letters on the wall in front of you."

"Yes, I see them."

Melody handed the instrument to Heather. "Cover your right eye and read the smallest line you can."

It surprised Heather when she realized she couldn't read the last two lines. Once again, the reality of her age crept in.

"This next part may be a little uncomfortable, but nothing will touch your eyes." Melody rotated a device in front of Heather that reminded her of an alien's metal face. "You'll need to lean forward, rest your chin in the indentation on the gray bar, and touch your forehead against the upper bar."

A series of clicks rang out as Melody spun dials. Redundant questions followed. "Which is more clear? This... or this?" After several minutes, Melody pulled the machine away. "We're almost finished." She reached into the pocket of her smock and pulled out a black cylinder, only a couple of inches thick. "This is a powerful magnifying glass. I won't touch your eye, but I will get very close. There's another machine I use after we dilate the eyes that gives me a better look, but since we're not dilating today, I'll just take a quick peek. With your good medical history, I'm sure there's nothing to worry about."

Heather noticed the slight smell of lavender body wash when Melody drew close, but no perfume.

The exam ended with the announcement, "That's all. You can sit back and relax." Dr. Melody smiled and said, "And we managed to get through before the cops broke down the door."

"Really?" asked Heather. "That's all there is?"

"If you've changed your mind and would like me to dilate your eyes and take a better look, I'll be glad to do it."

"No." She realized the force she'd put behind the word. "I mean, no thanks. Next time I'll have Jack drive me, or I'll call Uber like Steve does whenever he needs to go somewhere."

Melody went back to her computer. "You must do a lot of reading and computer work."

Heather picked up her computer and began tapping keys. "Every day. All day long. Why do you ask?"

"You've reached the point where you need reading glasses."

Heather looked away. "And I was teasing Jack about getting older."

"If you don't want to wear glasses, you can try contact lenses, but there's a big con in your case. You must touch them to your eye and sort of pinch them with your fingers to remove them. They also require some getting used to."

Heather shook her head. "The thought of anyone touching my eyes, even me, would make me break out in a cold sweat. There has to be something else."

"You'll either love the alternative, or hate it. Lasik surgery. It's safe and fast, with only a day or two recovery time in most cases. I can give you a referral to an ophthalmologist that I trusted with my eyes."

"Surgery? I'm not sure they could give me enough drugs to keep me on the table."

Melody pushed a button on her keyboard, and her printer came to life. "Another downside of surgery is, there's no guarantee you won't need reading glasses later on. All things considered, I'd say have a pair of glasses at your desk for work, and keep another pair in your purse for when you can't read the menu at a restaurant. You won't need them the rest of the time."

The door flew open, and Melody sprang to her feet. Heather stared at Detective Lowe. He took one look at her and glared. "What are you doing here?"

Melody gripped the paper and stepped toward Lowe. "Get out of my exam room."

"I'm Detective Lowe and I've been wasting my time trying to get a straight answer out of Steve Smiley. I want to know what you two are doing here."

Heather glared at him. "What did he tell you?"

"He said you were here to get your eyes examined. I've heard better lies from my dog."

Melody held up Heather's prescription to his face. "This is Ms. McBlythe's prescription for glasses I've just printed. I don't care who you are. You're rude and in violation of HIPPA laws. I'll not tolerate either in my clinic." She pointed to the hallway. "The waiting room is through that door. I'll be with you when I'm through with my patient."

Heather pushed the send button on her computer.

Lowe extended a clenched fist with an index finger, pointing at Melody. "You can talk to me now, or after I have an officer take you to the station."

Heather kept her tone firm and low. "In case you forgot, I'm an attorney, and Dr. Craddock is under no obligation to help you with your investigation. I doubt she'll be in much of a mood to talk to you now that you've threatened her. Perhaps you should speak with Detective Hall. He's already taken a statement from Dr. Craddock."

Melody handed Heather the prescription, but directed her next comment to Lowe. "That's Dr. Melody Craddock. Don't get me mixed up with my ex-husband."

Detective Lowe had his back to the hallway and didn't see Steve and Detective Hall approach. Steve spoke with reduced volume. "It's a good thing there are no other patients around. You three are making one heck of a racket."

"Hilarious, Smiley. How did you and your partner get here so fast?"

"Someone had to drive her to her eye appointment."

"You're a real comedian."

Steve placed both hands on top of his cane. "Why don't we all take a deep breath and stop wasting time?"

Detective Hall held up his cell phone. "Here are my notes from the interview with Dr. Melody. I'll get them on a witness statement and have her sign them tomorrow morning."

Lowe squinted at the words on the screen. "I want her signature on a statement today."

Melody spoke past Lowe to Detective Hall. "Make sure you use large print. The way he's squinting, he needs glasses."

Lowe pushed past Steve. "Come with me, Hall. We have work to do next door."

Melody spoke first after the door to the waiting room shut behind the two detectives. "What an unpleasant man."

"He's having a bad day," said Steve.

"Aren't we all?" Melody handed Heather her prescription. "You can get your glasses anywhere you want, even online, but I recommend a reputable shop with people who know how to adjust them properly."

A small smile crept across Steve's lips, enough to let Heather know he found the news of her needing glasses funny.

"If I hear one joke about having four eyes or how this will affect my love life, you'll get laxative in your coffee."

Steve held up a hand in surrender. "I think women who wear glasses look sexy."

"I bet Maggie didn't wear glasses."

"You'd lose that bet. Contacts most of the time, but glasses to read in bed. I thought she looked cute when she fell asleep reading and her glasses slid down her nose."

Leave it to Steve to surprise her again. As she pondered her future wearing glasses, he turned. "I'd hoped to spend more time next door, but that's off the table now. Melody, Detective Hall told me you can open your retail shop the day after tomorrow. Would it be possible for me and Heather to come back and interview your staff?"

"Sure. You can use the small office at the rear of the store."

"That reminds me. Detective Hall will come and get you in a little while. The cops need to know exactly what's missing from the file cabinet."

"Do you want me to call you after I've had a good look?"

"That would save Detective Hall a phone call."

Melody looked down the hall. "He seems like a decent guy."

"Most cops are," said Heather.

Steve added, "After their rough edges get knocked off."

11

Heather dropped her valise on the bar of her townhouse, went to her bedroom to put on shorts and a loose-fitting T-shirt, and started down the hall to go next door. While passing the kitchen, she heard Steve holler. "I hope you're in the mood for curry tonight. I ordered from the Indian place you like so much."

After giving a high five to an imaginary person, she shouted back a two-word response. "That's perfect." In a matter of seconds, she was out the door of her condo and sitting on Steve's couch, her lap filled with a purring cat.

"Did you have a productive afternoon?" asked Steve.

"Busy. I had to clear my schedule of almost everything so we could work on this case."

"Almost everything?"

Heather sensed a barb in the way Steve asked the question. "We don't really know if this is a murder case yet. Cleo Stanley could have tripped."

"It's being treated as one by Detective Hall."

"That's odd. Melody called me after we left her office. Detective Lowe hinted he wants to separate the burglary from the death of Cleo Stanley. That way, he has a simple burglary where nothing of real value is missing, and the death could be an accident. The cord to the vacuum cleaner wrapped around her feet supports that theory."

Steve interrupted her. "You're right about Lowe wanting to call the death an accident, but higher-ups rejected his assumptions. It seems Lowe's day got worse after he lied about calling in sick. His captain agreed with Hall's opinion that the coincidence of a burglary and a dead body on the same night was too much. That, and the injury to Mattie Arnold's eye after Dr. Chris put in the dilation drops all adds up to something too suspicious to ignore."

He kept talking. "Too many loose ends. How did the burglar get in? How did they get in the locked file cabinet? Lowe found no marks on it. Cleo only had keys to the front door. Then there's the possibility of someone targeting two optometrist's businesses, both owned by people with the same last name."

Steve took a drink from a tall glass of iced tea. "It must have been the last straw for the captain. Detective Lowe is off the case and assigned to desk duty pending a disciplinary hearing."

"What a relief. I wasn't looking forward to tip-toeing around Lowe until we get this sorted."

"Speaking of missing documents. They were tax records for the last five years."

Max moved from Heather's lap to the end of the couch, circled twice, and lay down.

"I heard," said Heather. "Any ideas on why someone would want to break into a business that sells glasses and steal their tax records?"

"The answer's trying to come to the surface, but I can't grab it yet." He shrugged. "Oh well, a tasty supper will either activate the brain or put me to sleep."

Right on cue, a knock came from the front door. Steve spoke as Heather rose. "I paid and added the tip."

"Good. I didn't bring my purse."

It didn't take long before they sat at the kitchen table with steaming bowls of Chicken Tikka Masala in front of them, with slabs of naan in hand, ready to dip and scoop the savory dish.

After several bites without talking, Steve asked, "What makes this stuff so good?"

Heather had to chew and swallow before she could answer. "It's the combination of flavors. Chunks of chicken in a sauce of plain yogurt, garam masala, serrano peppers, tomatoes, and heavy cream. It reminds me of a trip I took down the Ganges River as a child. That's where I fell in love with this dish and learned to eat it with naan. It's very efficient to eat without a fork."

Steve held up a piece of naan. "It feels like a puffy tortilla, but tastes sort of like bread, only better." He took a quick bite. "What did you call this dish with chicken? A gram of masala?"

Heather shook her head and swallowed. "Garam means hot. Masala is spices. Any combination of ground and sometimes toasted spices can make up masala. Think of it as a Colonel Sanders secret recipe of eleven herbs and spices. In India, that combination is a masala. There are hundreds of masalas. Since they put serrano peppers in this dish, it's called garam masala. A hot, or spicy, mixture of spices."

Steve dipped a chunk of naan in a hearty red sauce but didn't bring it to his lips. "What gives naan such a distinct taste?"

"Yogurt and yeast. Traditionally it's baked in a scorching hot oven, then slathered with clarified butter and sprinkled with minced cilantro."

Steve took a bite of naan soaked in flavor. "Almost as good as chicken fried steak."

Heather kept her head down and scooped another bite of chicken tikka masala. Some comments from Steve didn't deserve a response.

With bowls and plates placed in the sink and the coffee pot sputtering behind him, Steve placed his hands flat on the table. "I was a bit surprised by the level of animosity Melody expressed toward Chris today."

Heather rose to get mugs down from the cabinet. "Jack said it was a rough divorce."

"What about Jack's relationship with Chris?"

Heather poured the coffee. "They don't get together that often. Chris was a last-minute addition to the cruise when another friend had to cancel. There's still something about that guy that doesn't sit right with me, but I can't put my finger on it."

"Do you smell a rat?"

"Something like that. In college, I did a study on intuition. There's a ton of information on it that ranges from psycho-babble, to religious writings, to credible experiments with double-blind studies."

"What conclusions did you reach?"

"That's a tough one to answer, and it makes me sound like a mystic."

"Give it your best shot."

Heather delivered the coffee and took a seat. "Let's say I walk into a crowded room of people I don't know. Within a few minutes, I'll either gravitate to certain people or steer clear of them. It's somewhere between a feeling and a knowing." She put air quotes around the word knowing and then realized she'd done it for no reason.

"A gut instinct?" asked Steve.

"Same thing, and my gut tells me not to trust Chris."

Steve rubbed his chin. "Did you feel that way before you spent time with Melody?"

"It wasn't as strong, but an unease comes over me every time Jack tells me he's playing golf with Chris."

"Interesting. Maggie could always spot them, too."

"Them?"

"Liars. They didn't have to say a word, and she'd pick them out."

"Could she spot anything else?"

"Unfaithful husbands."

Heather chuckled. "I bet that kept you from checking out anything more than the produce at the grocery store."

"That's good. I'll have to put it in a story."

While she took her first sip of coffee, Steve kept talking. "Speaking of writing, Kate called today for a progress report on the short story."

"Have you worked on it lately?"

"I told her we're working a fresh case. Of course, she had to hear all about it. She laughed when I asked if it had potential for a story."

"She didn't like the idea?"

"She loved it for a cozy mystery, but not for a police procedural. She thought the setting for the murder sounded original, but the protagonist needed to be a grandmother with poor vision. Also, she said it would work better if there was an emphasis on baking, and a cat or two who played a role in solving the crime. I told her to take the idea and run with it. I draw the line at cats solving crimes."

"What did she say to that?"

"She's going to start a new series with it, and put it under the pen name she uses for her other cozy mysteries."

"I thought she wrote historical romance novels."

"That's her primary focus, but those take a lot of research. She uses cozy mysteries to clear her brain."

Heather wanted to keep Steve talking about Kate, but when he stood, she knew that conversation was over. She settled the question about who would wash dishes by saying, "You cooked. I clean. Enjoy your coffee and we'll talk about how you want to proceed with the case."

Steve didn't argue, and in a few minutes, she joined him, sitting yoga style on the couch near his chair. Max had already assumed one of his favorite spots, on Steve's lap, receiving all the strokes a cat could want.

"I want you to concentrate on Sandi Fields, the store manager for Chris's retail store," said Steve. "You have a perfect excuse to stop by and try on glasses. This time you don't have to bend the truth."

Heather groaned. "I'll do it, but the thought of wearing glasses almost makes me break out in hives. Besides, I'd rather buy from Melody than support Chris."

"Who said you have to make a purchase? Get to know Sandi and learn what you can about her relationship with Chris. Also, see what you can find out about the true financial state of his two businesses."

"Those are both nice-looking properties. He must have sunk a lot of money into them."

Steve pulled the wooden handle on the side of his recliner and raised his feet. "What did your father teach you? It's not how much you make, it's how much you keep that really matters."

"That's one of a hundred mantras he lives by. Another is to use OPM. Other people's money. I bet Chris borrowed as much as the bank let him."

A few seconds of silence passed before Steve spoke again. "Talking about your father brought something to mind. How's your mother today?"

"Holy smoke," said Heather as she uncrossed her legs. "First, it's my eyes and now my memory. I'll be back after I call her."

Steve chuckled. "You can call, but she may not answer."

Heather gave Steve a squinted stare. "How do you know?"

"Your father called asking about you. I gave him a quick rundown on the case we're working. He said your mother had some sort of civic event to attend this evening."

Heather stood with her mouth open. After a few seconds, she placed her hands on her hips. "Are there any other updates on my life I need to know?"

"A couple. Jack had to work late. He's hitting a bucket of golf balls before he goes home." Steve paused. "Also, Cora has an appointment with a cardiologist next Tuesday. You're invited to go along if you want to."

Heather pulled both hands down her face and moaned. "I have to be the most self-absorbed person in the world."

"Nonsense," said Steve.

"Jack deserves better."

"So did Maggie, but she chose me."

Silence took over until Steve said, "While you're with Sandi Fields tomorrow, I'll have a chat with Dora Chen, Melody's assistant. You can drop me off and I'll call Uber to get home."

Heather turned toward the front door. "Thanks for supper. I need to call Father. Mother didn't sound very peppy the last time I spoke with her."

Steve held up a hand to wave goodbye. "Max isn't used to you being home so early. He may think his internal clock broke."

"Send him over whenever you want. I'm sure he understands what you say."

Steve continued stroking Max. "Come for breakfast in the morning after you finish your workout at the gym. We'll talk more about Sandi Fields and Dora Chen. I may even have another talk with Chris tomorrow."

"He's all yours," said Heather as she reached for the doorknob.

12

———————

S teve's invitation for Heather to come for breakfast meant one of two things: either he would drag out some boxes of cereal, or he'd make toast. All past attempts at a more substantive breakfast resulted in runny eggs and blackened bacon.

Since no boxes of cereal awaited Heather as she arrived, she put on an apron and dredged the refrigerator for suitable ingredients. This proved to be no problem as Steve always had a better stocked larder than she did.

"Scrambled, fried, or poached eggs?" asked Heather.

"Fried."

"Bacon, sausage, or ham?"

"I prefer bacon this morning. You'll need the grease to make gravy."

Heather pulled open the door to the refrigerator. "I see you ordered a couple of packages of the extra buttery bake-and-serve biscuits. You must want the cardiologist's special."

"Keep looking. There's yogurt and fresh fruit to balance it out."

"I'm not sure it works that way, but thanks for getting me something you knew I'd eat."

Steve sat at the bar and sipped his coffee. "Speaking of cardiologists, any update on Jack's mother?"

Heather pulled plates out of a cabinet. "Jack said she wants to cancel the appointment. He threw a wobbly and insisted she keep it."

"He threw a what?"

"It's a phrase I picked up in south England. Instead of throwing a fit, some Brits say they throw a wobbly. I used it once and Jack picked up on it. It's an inside joke between us. Whenever one of us is upset, whoever isn't having the meltdown will say, 'Wobbly alert!' It's hard to throw a fit if you're laughing."

Steve's little paunch of a belly jiggled as he said wobbly three times. "Great word. I'll have to remember to use it."

Bacon sizzled in the skillet as the aroma of biscuits baking filled the kitchen. Thanks to a cooking class she'd taken in Paris, Heather timed everything, so the plates arrived at the table with the selections at the perfect serving temperature. As usual, Steve fell upon the meal with gusto and showered her with compliments.

She allowed him to get halfway through before interrupting with a question. "Are you sure you want to split up this morning?"

"That was my original plan, but let's stick together. We'll start at the eyewear store with Sandi. If Chris is at his office, we'll stop in and clarify a thing or two."

"Why wouldn't he be there?"

Steve put his fork down. "I'm not sure if it's a feeling, or if my knower is going off."

Heather lowered her fork. "Are you making fun of me?"

He held up his hands. "Don't throw a wobbly."

Heather groaned. "I've created another monster." She shook her head and asked, "What do you have planned for us to do this afternoon?"

"Find out how many lies Chris and his employees tell us this morning."

"AT LEAST THE NEWS CREW ISN'T BACK THIS MORNING," SAID Heather, as she parked between Chris's practice and his retail store.

"Are there many cars?" asked Steve.

"Only a few parked away from the building."

Steve nodded in a way that showed he approved. "It's early. Do you see Chris's car?"

Heather swiveled her head. "Didn't Melody say he drives a Porsche Boxster?"

"He did at one time, but that was when he and Melody were married." Heather pulled out her phone and told it to call Jack.

Jack issued a greeting he'd developed for her. "Good morning, gorgeous."

"Good morning, handsome."

"Is this business or pleasure?"

"Business. Steve's listening. We're at Chris's clinic. What kind of car does he drive?"

"A Porsche 911."

"Is it new?"

"She got the house. He needed something with four doors so he could pick up the kids for visitation. It's a four-door rocket on wheels and a chick-magnet."

In her mind's eye she could see Chris trying to impress a woman twenty years his junior. "What color is the woman-trap?"

"Silver."

"Thanks. Call me tonight."

"I have a better idea. Why don't you come to my place for supper?"

Before Heather could answer, Steve spoke. "She'll be there. What time?"

"I'll be home at five thirty. If she wants to let herself in earlier and do laundry, that would be great."

"Don't look for me before six thirty," said Heather. "Got to run. There are bad guys to catch."

She hit the end call icon and looked at Steve. "Melody got all the equity in an expensive home and Chris settled for a depreciating asset. It's obvious he's an optometrist and not a financial adviser."

Steve rubbed his chin, but said nothing.

Heather took his hand and placed it on her arm. "Let's get you inside before you complain about the heat."

He asked, "Did you bring your prescription?"

"I thought you said I didn't have to buy anything."

"You don't, but Sandi will need to see it."

"Why?"

Steve let out a huff of exasperation. "You still have so much to learn. Not all frames accommodate certain prescriptions. It will be one of the first things Sandi will ask you for."

Heather let out a soft sigh. "This is all unfamiliar territory."

Once they walked into air-conditioned comfort, Heather stopped and whispered, "We're the only customers, and Sandi's the only worker."

Steve whispered back, "Find out how many sales people they have."

"Welcome," came the chirpy voice from the back of the room. Sandi came toward them with full red lips parted to show off ultra-white teeth.

Heather extended her hand. "I'm Heather McBlythe and this is my business partner, Steve Smiley. We saw you at Dr. Craddock's office next door, but Chris didn't introduce us."

"I've heard your name before. Don't you date Jack Blackstock?"

"That's right. Steve and I are private detectives helping Chris concerning the death at Dr. Melody's business."

Heather purposefully left out the full extent of their involvement in both cases, at least for now.

Sandi tucked the dazzling smile behind lipstick. "Wasn't that the most horrible thing? Who in their right mind would want to harm Cleo?"

"Did you know her well?" asked Steve.

"When I managed that store, I made it a point to be first in the showroom each morning. Cleo did a good job, but she'd sometimes fall asleep in the back office after she finished her work." She paused and turned her head. "Did Chris send you over to ask me questions about Cleo?"

Steve placed both hands on the top of his cane. "Heather has a prescription she needs help with."

The smile came back full force. "If you let me see it, I'll help you find glasses that will make you look even more lovely than you already are."

The smile left Sandi when she saw the letterhead and signature of Dr. Melody Craddock. "Oh," she said, as if looking at a flat tire on her car. "I thought Chris said you were his patient."

Heather kept her voice buoyant. "I wasn't intending on Dr. Melody examining my eyes, but things got complicated."

Steve added, "We needed to buy a little time and all of Dr. Melody's morning appointments were cancelled."

Heather took her turn. "It wasn't planned, but it might work out where Chris will still get my business."

"And speaking of business," said Steve. "We're helping Dr. Chris find out how contaminated eyedrops found their way into his treatment room. What can you tell us about Mattie Arnold?"

Blond hair moved side to side as Sandi shook her head. "Poor Mattie. Her mother first brought her to Dr. Chris when she was in middle school. I helped her set the fashion trend in her school for years."

Sandi looked at the prescription again. "I'm still not sure why what happened at Dr. Melody's retail store has anything to do with you not using Chris?"

"Silly me," said Heather. "I didn't tell you. After I took a quick look at where Cleo died, I bopped back to Melody's office, where I'd left Steve." She looked around the showroom and pretended to share a secret. "I hate to admit it, but I'm a sucker for a bargain. Dr. Melody offered to give me a free eye exam, and I took her up on it."

The muscles in Sandi's jaws flexed and then relaxed. The smile came back. "We'll make sure you get a good deal too. In fact, I'll give you our preferred customer discount on your first pair, and the sunglasses will be half price."

With what looked like hundreds of frames to choose from, no other sales staff in sight, and a marked absence of customers, Heather and Steve had Sandi all to themselves.

After rejecting five selections, Heather eased into her questions as Steve stayed to the side, silent as a rock. "You're so patient," said Heather. "How long have you been in this profession?"

"I started a long time ago. Dr. Craddock hired me."

"Which Dr. Craddock?"

Sandi's sculpted eyebrows moved together for a fraction of a section. "Dr. Melody. The retail store was her idea."

"Of course," said Heather. "Was that when she was in college to become an optometrist?"

"She was halfway through her degree. Dr. Chris ran his practice alone then."

Heather tried on some gaudy plastic frames in primary colors and cringed. She pointed to the empty desks where sales clerks should be. "I guess business is slow this early."

"It picks up after lunch. There're three others, but I'm the sales manager."

Heather wondered if the others worked full or part-time.

Steve came out of his shell, which gave Heather a chance to plan other questions. "Heather didn't notice Chris's car when we drove up. Do you know if he'll open the clinic today?"

"Do you need to talk to him?"

The question seemed odd and protective. Steve responded with something to rattle Sandi. "Since he also hired us to help Melody, we need to give him a progress update."

Sandi's toothy smile came back. "Isn't that just like him, to want to do something nice?"

The response sounded like something written in a script and rehearsed. Too bad she wasted another smile on Steve.

"Let's try on the leopard print frames," said Sandi. "They might go with your hair."

Heather didn't know so many adverbs and adjectives existed to complement hunks of metal, plastic, and glass. Sandi deserved credit: she could schmooze a customer.

"Try these," said Sandy.

"I don't think so. My cat, Max, might be jealous if I try to look like his mother." Heather moved on to the next display. "I've been admiring your tan. I'm white as a bowl of snow. Do you have a tanning bed at home?"

"Nothing like that. I'm a bit of a sun-worshiper, so the pool at our apartment complex is where you'll find me on my days off."

A question leapt into Heather's mind, but she needed to be careful about how she approached Sandi with it. "The only time I got such a perfect tan was when I spent two weeks cruising the Mediterranean."

Sandi took the bait. "I know what you mean about getting an even tan on a cruise ship. I sleep until eleven, eat a quick bite, then spend the afternoon on the lido deck by the pool. Listening to music, sipping drinks with little umbrellas, and turning over every twenty minutes is my idea of heaven."

"Do you cruise often?"

Sandi glanced at the door as if someone might come in, intending to eavesdrop on her conversation. "Don't tell anyone, but if things work out the way I hope, there may be a career change in my future and I'll be able to cruise much more often."

To keep her on the same topic without sounding pushy, Heather raised her eyebrows and used a single word. "Oh?"

"My heart is set on becoming a travel agent. They know all the ins and outs."

Heather leaned in. "Your secret is safe with me."

A smiling woman on a poster looked down at Heather as she moved to the next row of frames. Sandi took note and said, "If it weren't for the hair color, the woman could be your twin."

Heather looked again at the poster. The model wore nondescript metal frames with what looked like ultra-thin lenses.

Heather pointed. "There. Those are the ones I want."

"Excellent choice," said Sandi as she reached for the frames. "Try these on and see what you think."

Heather examined a reflection of her new look from several angles. The woman on the poster seemed to smile her approval. "If I have to wear glasses, these will do."

While completing the sales process on her computer, Sandi began by pointing out upgrades. Heather sidestepped the sales pitch by pointing to the options at the bottom of a laminated sheet. "Give me the deluxe package."

Sandi flashed another smile. "I wish all my customers were as decisive as you. You know what you want and you get it."

Heather knew how to interpret that line. What Sandi meant was, "I wish all my customers were as easy as you."

While typing in all the details of the sale, Sandi returned to the prior conversation. "It's nice having Galveston so close, and there're different cruise lines and ships to choose from, but I'm ready to try something new, maybe a little more upscale." She leaned forward. "I was jealous when you said you cruised the Mediterranean."

"When was the last time you cruised?" asked Steve.

"A few months ago. It was a five-day trip to a couple of ports in Mexico. I stayed on board and soaked up the sun."

Steve nudged Heather with his elbow. "Isn't that the cruise you wanted to go on?"

"I wish I had."

"It wasn't anything special, but it was still nice to get away from here for a while." Sandi looked from the computer screen to Heather, summarized the order and asked how she wanted to pay.

Heather handed over her credit card. A few minutes later she and Steve walked out with a receipt for two pair of reading glasses and another pair of sunglasses.

Once outside, Heather pulled up short of Dr. Chris's door. "How many lies did she tell?"

"Not many, and not big ones. It's our client I'm not so sure about. There's something under the surface about what happened to Mattie Arnold and Cleo's death. The longer I think about it, the more convinced I am those two events are linked."

"Do you think Chris is involved?"

Steve placed his hand on the top of his cane. "It's something deeper than that. Chris may be a terrible businessman, a lousy husband and father, and perhaps a habitual liar, but I can't see him harming a patient or sabotaging his business. He doesn't strike me as a killer, either."

Heather let out a huff. "You talk to Chris. I need to speak with a certain attorney named Jack and get the full story of what happened on that cruise."

Steve spoke with confidence. "You can trust Jack."

"Wasn't it a former president that said, 'Trust, but verify?'"

"I think he also said, 'Don't throw a wobbly.'"

Heather sputtered out a laugh.

Steve held out his hand. "I may be wrong about that last quote. Let's see if Chris is coming in today."

Heather noticed a car turning into the parking lot. "A shiny silver Porsche is rolling up."

"Our luck seems to be holding."

13

Chris approached with a set of keys in hand. "I hope you haven't been out here in the sun very long."

Steve waved off the question. "We were next door. Heather ordered glasses. You're right about Sandi. She could sell sand in the Sahara."

Heather piled on with, "I hope you don't mind, but while we were at Melody's yesterday, she gave me an eye exam. I thought I'd make it up to you by buying my glasses from your store today."

He twisted the key in the lock. "No apology needed. The retail side is where most of the profit comes from." He pulled open the door and allowed her and Steve to pass in front of him.

Steve spoke next. "Since you opened the door with a key, I take it you're not open for business today."

"Half-day only. I thought the news crew might show up again this morning. Jack issued a release to the press this morning. He informed them the substance found in the eye drops wasn't acid, but the diluted juice from a hot pepper. If I'd known it was capsaicin that burned her eye, I would have used milk to irrigate instead of water. It has a protein in it that helps stop the burning sensation."

Steve responded, "That tells us Detective Hall got the lab results back. It makes sense that you had to pin Mattie down to do the irrigation. When I had my sight, I accidentally rubbed my eye after chopping a couple of jalapenos. It felt like someone put a burning cigarette on it."

"That's what capsaicin does, burns like fire. If you'd used milk, you would have experienced relief sooner. Even drinking milk helps."

"So, it's official? There's no permanent damage to Mattie's eye?"

Chris smiled. "I spoke with the ophthalmologist this morning. Capsaicin can cause blindness in strong concentrations, but the amount in the eye drops wasn't high enough."

Heather added, "That still leaves the question of who put it in the bottle and why."

The smile left Chris. "I have no answer to either question. The only people who work in this office are the receptionist and me."

"Can we speak with her?"

"She's from a temp agency. I called and canceled her for today."

Steve put both hands on top of his cane. "Has this temp receptionist worked for you very long?"

"Only a week. I hate to say it, but she's not working out. I'm going to ask for a replacement."

"Does she know yet?"

"Oh, no. I always let the agency deliver the bad news."

Heather asked, "Did she have access to the eye drops?"

Chris shook his head. "I never saw her go any farther down the hall than to my office. The restrooms are right by her office, so she wouldn't have a reason to be in or near the exam rooms. To tell the truth, she's a lazy little thing and seemed pretty self-absorbed. I can't imagine her expending the energy to sabotage my business, whether for her own reasons or someone else's."

Chris ran a hand down his freshly shaved face. "Are you thinking this might have been an inside job?"

Steve laughed. "You've been watching too many cop shows. As things stand, it's more likely someone with a sick sense of humor contaminated a single bottle at the factory or along the supply chain."

Heather asked, "Did you hear from the manufacturer?"

"Not a peep."

She glanced around the empty waiting room. "They're hoping to keep their company name out of the news. I'm sure if they need to know anything, they'll go through the police."

Chris followed Heather's lead in looking at the empty waiting room. "This didn't come at a good time."

Heather turned back to Chris. "Why would now be worse than any other?"

"I know a guy who helps owners sell businesses. While I examined his eyes, he talked about some of his clients. No names, only the type of businesses."

"Did he offer to sell either of yours?"

Chris shook his head. "No, but it got me to thinking about it. I'm no expert on buying and selling, but right after a potential scandal doesn't seem the best time to put out a 'for sale' sign."

"It's not," said Heather. "My advice, if you want to sell, is to put all your effort into these two businesses for at least another year. Your profit-and-loss statement will be your best sales tool."

Chris shuffled his feet. "You sound like my ex-wife. She took care of the money end of the business while we were married."

Steve took one of his hands off the top of his cane. "Was it her idea to open a retail store beside your practice?"

"Yeah. How'd you know?"

"Lucky guess."

Heather knew Steve well enough to know he didn't make a lucky guess. It surprised her when he didn't pursue the matter.

"Is there anything else?" Chris motioned to the receptionist desk. "I need to get started rescheduling appointments. The receptionist made a real hash out of it the day they hauled Mattie out of here. Oh, well. I'll have it all straightened out by the time I leave tonight."

Steve took a step toward the door and stopped. "By the way, Heather and Sandi hit it off this morning. She told us about going on the same cruise you went on this spring. It's a shame Heather had a murder case to work the week of the cruise. If she'd gone, Sandi would have had someone besides a bunch of guys to talk to."

Chris didn't hesitate. "She knows how to keep herself entertained. You wouldn't recognize her on board a ship. Misses breakfast every day, stays by the pool all afternoon, eats something from the buffet, then it's all night in the casino until they throw her out."

"That doesn't sound like a restful vacation."

"It wasn't for her, but us four guys came back in good shape. Did Jack tell you we had a contest to see who would spend the least amount of money?"

"I heard something about it, but not who won."

"I did," said Chris, with pride sprinkling his words. "Sandi knows every travel hack in the book. She contacted the cruise line and got us upgraded to better rooms at no charge. Then she talked them into giving us onboard credits. I let the others have mine. Finally, Sandi told me some of the ways you can earn prizes or more onboard credits. They try to get people to take part in games, quizzes, karaoke, and shopping seminars. By the time I did everything on the ship's schedule for five days, I'd earned enough to reimburse the guys for my share of the cabin with plenty left over."

Steve chuckled. "I never heard of anyone going on a cruise and coming home better off financially. Thanks for your time, Chris."

Heather opened the door leading to the parking lot. Once they were past any chance of being overheard, she whispered. "You're a sly one, Detective Smiley."

"I have to admit, that one caught me flat-footed. I would have guessed Chris spent the cruise helping Sandi smear suntan lotion on those hard-to-reach places."

With the SUV running and the air conditioner cooling, Heather asked, "Is that all the people you want to talk to this morning?"

"Let's go back to Dr. Melody's. Her assistant wasn't at work when Cleo Stanley died and we need to find out why she picked that particular day to take off."

AFTER CHECKING IN WITH A VERY BUSY DR. MELODY, Heather and Steve went in search of Dora Chen, one of her two assistants. On the way down a hallway, Heather almost ran into a short, dark-haired woman coming out of an exam room.

"Who are you, and how can I help you?" she asked with a thick Asian accent.

"I'm Heather McBlythe and this is Steve Smiley. We're assisting the police with their investigation. Dr. Melody told us we could come back here and speak with you. Is there somewhere private we can sit and have a chat?"

It was then Heather noticed the woman blinked her eyes more often than normal.

"As long as Dr. Melody said so. Come to my office." She walked ahead of them with shoulders pinned back and head erect until she came to a doorway. She stood back, gave a slight bow, and extended an arm with palm held up. "You may sit wherever you like."

Heather took a look into the small space. Its size led her to believe in its former life it was a broom closet. It held all the necessary furnishings and equipment, but the size matched that of their diminutive hostess. Steve held his cane straight up and allowed Heather to direct him to a chair. She described the room, which didn't seem to bother Dora. She waited with hands folded in front of her until Heather stopped talking, then eased down onto a chair as if she wore a back brace under her scrubs.

Steve began the conversation while Heather counted the time between eye blinks.

"Thanks for speaking with us today. I hope you're feeling better."

Her head didn't move. "You assume because I wasn't here at the time of the incident, I was off sick. That is not the case. I had a washing machine delivered and had no one but myself to let delivery persons into my apartment."

Heather stopped counting the intervals between Dora's eye blinks. Two seconds, every time.

Steve kept talking in his easy, calm manner. "The last time I had an appliance delivered, they wouldn't give me a time. All they said was it would be in the morning. It didn't arrive until three in the afternoon."

"They weren't that precise for me," said Dora. "I had to be home all day." Dora kept her head straight. "Are you police?"

"Private detectives," said Steve, still in a casual tone. "We understand you used to work for Dr. Chris before they divorced. Is that right?"

"Yes."

"When did you hear what happened at the retail store next door?"

"I heard on the news."

"What about the tainted eye drops at Dr. Chris's practice?"

"Yes. I heard about both on the news."

"Dr. Chris and Dr. Melody asked us to look into both cases."

Dora nodded that she understood. "I heard."

Steve folded his collapsible cane as she spoke. "Did you know the victim, Cleo Stanley?"

The blinks continued at the same steady pace. "She cleaned the clinic first, then the store that sells eyeglasses. I never spoke to her."

"How long have you worked with Doctors Chris and Melody?"

"I started nine months before they divorced."

"Why didn't you want to keep working with Dr. Chris?"

This question produced a double blink. "It's part of my culture to be wise when making long term decisions. I weighed my choices and chose Dr. Melody."

Heather made an observation. "I've always admired your culture. Did you find adjusting to this country difficult?"

She nodded. "Hard at first, but my country also teaches patience and hard work."

"What type of work did you do before you came to America?"

"Much the same. I worked in an eye clinic."

Steve took over again. "Do you know anyone who might have wanted to harm Cleo Stanley?"

"No."

"What's your opinion of Dr. Melody?"

"I don't know how to answer. Please be more specific."

"Is she a good optometrist?"

"Yes."

"Is she a talented businesswoman?"

"Very good. Very smart. A good brain for business."

"Did you know she started the retail store while she attended college to be an optometrist?"

Two more quick blinks. "I learned that after I was hired."

As he was apt to do, Steve changed subjects. "Do you think Dr. Melody or someone at this clinic tampered with the drops that burned Mattie Arnold's eye?"

This question earned three quick blinks. "I don't know how. Mattie Arnold wasn't injured here." She paused. "I don't understand why or how people can do such things."

"We know Dr. Melody helped Dr. Chris by giving him supplies when he opened his businesses. Do you think someone tampered with the drops before they came to this clinic?"

"I have difficulty with that question. I was taught to deal with facts, not speculation."

"I agree," said Steve as he rose. "Thank you for your time. Do you mind if we contact you if we have any further questions?"

"As long as you have permission from Dr. Melody, I'll answer all questions to the best of my ability."

Heather led Steve down the hallway and across the waiting area. Once outside, she asked, "Did you get anything useful out of Dora?"

"Nothing about the contaminated eye drops."

"What about the death of Cleo Stanley?"

"She dodged only one question, but sometimes it's the thing that appears irrelevant that ends up being a key bit of information."

Steve's phone announced an incoming call from Dr. Chris. He put it on speaker after salutations were traded. "I'd like to talk to you more about how the case is progressing. Perhaps we can meet over dinner tonight and go over everything. How does Chez Pierre sound? My treat."

Heather leaned toward Steve and projected her voice. "Here's a piece of business advice for you, Chris. Don't spend money on fancy meals until you can afford them." She straightened her posture and increased her volume. "We have nothing new to report to you at this time."

Chris responded with a laugh. "I get it, you're hot on the trail and don't want distractions. I'll let you get back to it then."

After ending the call, Steve put his phone in his pocket. "I think your advice fell on deaf ears."

"Seems it did."

As she led Steve to the car, she thought about the short conversation. She understood why Jack counted Chris as a friend. He could be a charmer.

Once in her SUV, she turned her head to face Steve and asked, "What's next?"

"Lunch, including a debriefing on the two interviews. Then home to dictate notes, and, most important, a nice long nap."

"It all sounds good except the nap. I'll use that time to call Jack's mom."

"Good for you," said Steve. "If you have time, call Kate and tell her how the case is progressing. A different perspective might help her with plotting the story."

Heather started the car and considered Steve's request that she call Kate. What was he up to?

14

———————

It didn't surprise Heather when Steve chose a restaurant known for serving portions large enough to feed two people. He'd eat half for lunch and take home plenty for a future meal. She'd learned over the years to follow his lead with the super-sized entrees. Steve could have his choice of a repeat of his dinner or the rest of her meal for variety. Leftovers ranked as one of his favorite food groups. He claimed to not be a miser, but rather, a faithful practitioner of thrift.

While waiting for his order of black-skillet southern-fried chicken and her order of meat loaf with assorted vegetables, they sipped iced tea. "Is it sweet enough for you?" she asked.

"Perfect. The spoon might stand up by itself if they put in any more sugar. I don't see how you can stand to drink yours without something to sweeten it."

Heather didn't respond to the comment. She knew the agenda Steve wanted to follow, so she got down to business. "Sandi Fields. What are your thoughts on her?"

"She's the biggest surprise of the day for me. No matter what Chris said, I thought for sure she was the *other woman* who wedged her way between him and Melody and led to their divorce."

"They had a fling." Heather voice carried a stab of condemnation.

"True, but Chris claimed it was a one-off, and he said it didn't happen until after the divorce. He and Sandi were on the same cruise, but went their separate ways. Jack said he never saw them together." Steve ran his fingers down the side of his glass. "Of course, that doesn't mean Jack kept close tabs on them."

Heather was still skeptical, but didn't belabor the point. Her mind shifted from Chris's businesses to Melody's. "I'm surprised by how much more prosperous Melody's retail store and practice are than Chris's. She has a full complement of salespeople on the retail side and two assistants doing refractions. I got a copy of the stolen tax returns from her accountant late yesterday afternoon."

"How did you get those?"

"I didn't tell you?" Heather had a hard time keeping a straight face. Several times over the years, he'd played this game of keeping a thing or two to himself during an investigation. He claimed it helped her think, and dig, deeper. This was payback.

"I thought I told you. Detective Hall and I went to Melody's CPA's office late yesterday afternoon. We talked her into making copies for Hall without a subpoena."

Steve put his forearms on the table and leaned over. "You win this round. Tell me what you learned."

"Melody works hard and smart. If I thought she'd sell at a decent price, I'd buy both businesses."

Steve leaned back. "Two optometrists with nearly identical floor plans for their practices and stores. Melody gets wealthy while Chris struggles to make ends meet."

Heather shrugged. "That's the way of business. There's no reason why Chris can't turn his around if he wants to."

Steve rubbed his chin. "I believe you hit on the problem."

"What do you mean?"

With hands folded, Steve explained. "Chris trained to be an optometrist and made a decent living at it. Melody wanted more, so she not only became an optometrist, but opened a retail store while raising children."

"Are you blaming her for their marriage falling apart?"

Steve shook his head. "Not at all. It's Chris who had the problem. He couldn't handle large amounts of money when it came too quick. He did stupid things."

Heather bought time to ponder Steve's words by taking a drink of iced tea. She settled the glass on a cardboard trivet. "Do you think one of his stupid decisions was to break into Melody's business and steal her tax returns?"

"Give me a motive."

Heather thought for a minute. "That stolen information could mean the difference in hiring a family law attorney or not. If he's broke and she's wallowing in money, he could petition the court for a reduction in child support. He'd get it, too."

Steve nodded. "That's the only reason I haven't written him off my list of suspects."

"Is Melody still on the list?"

"At first, I eliminated her from the suspects. Now I'm not so sure. She'd be off the list if it weren't for the hatred she has toward Chris. I wish I knew why."

"That's easy," said Heather. "Some women take a dim view of their husbands having an affair. We don't know if Sandi was the only one."

"Good point."

"Do you want me to interview Sandi again?"

Steve leaned back. "I believe you'd get more out of her than I would."

Heather watched as a server approached with their orders. "I'll put her on my list of people to call this afternoon." She reconsidered her last statement. "On second thought, I'll show up at her workplace tomorrow. If I'm any judge of character, she arrives at work thirty minutes early."

With hot fried chicken in front of him, the only acknowledgment Steve gave was a caveman's grunt. His desire to speak didn't return until Heather slid his left-overs into a styrofoam carryout container after he ordered a slice of pecan pie and coffee. "What's your impression of Dora Chen?"

Heather had her glass of water to her lips, but hadn't taken a sip yet. She lowered it to the table. "She's difficult to read, but she does something unusual with her eyes. She blinks every two seconds. On a couple of occasions, she varied the number of blinks."

"Interesting. What do you make of it?"

"I thought about it while you moaned and groaned over your chicken."

"Couldn't help it. Something magical happens when they fry chicken in a big cast iron skillet."

"I don't count having to see a cardiologist as magical."

"Back to Dora Chen and the mystery of the blinking eyes," said Steve. "What did you conclude?"

Heather had to wait while Steve's pie and their coffee arrived. Once delivered, she said, "Dora impressed me as someone who leads a very precise, regimented life. There wasn't one speck of dust in her office and everything had its place. She even irons her scrubs."

"What does that have to do with her blinking every two seconds?"

Heather ran a finger over the rim of her coffee cup. "It's possible she trained herself to blink that often to keep her eyes moist. I use drops because I stare at my computer all day and don't blink enough."

Steve found the clean fork the server brought, took his first bite of pie, and thoroughly chewed it. "Do you think the times she varied the blinks it was something like a poker tell?"

"It's possible. I recorded the entire interview. You can listen to it when we get home." Heather took a sip of coffee. "Who's next on your list of suspects?"

"There could be several more. Sandi Fields was the manager of the eyeglass store when Chris and Melody were together. She left when he did. That could have left competition for the job as store manager."

Heather interrupted, "That's the job Bryson Wayne has now."

"Right. I heard Cindy Green was particularly upset at not getting the manager's job."

"Where did you hear that?"

Steve tried not to smile. "Didn't I tell you? I called Detective Hall yesterday evening. He told me Cindy had seniority over Bryson and she thought Melody should have promoted her to store manager."

Heather held up a hand. "Stop right there, Steve Smiley. Did you say you called Hall last night?"

"Uh-huh."

"I was with him yesterday afternoon. Why didn't he tell me about Cindy Green being on the outs with Bryson Wayne?"

Steve grinned. "For the same reason you didn't tell me you and Hall got copies from the CPA yesterday afternoon while I slept."

Heather shut her eyes for several seconds as anger mixed with frustration. She opened them to see Steve shoving another bite of pie in his mouth. "You knew we went to get Melody's tax records, didn't you?"

"Uh-huh."

"And you strung me along by pretending you didn't know about it."

"Uh-huh."

Heather's coffee cup made a loud thunk when she brought it down to the table harder than she should have.

Steve only chuckled. "I hope you didn't chip the cup."

She ground out the next three sentences. "It's fine. I'm fine. Everything and everyone are fine."

"Kate's fine, too," said Steve. "In fact, she sold one of my short stories to a magazine."

It took Heather a moment to realize her mouth had hinged

open. "When did this happen, and why didn't you tell me you'd finished something?"

"It's only a short story. I'll be lucky to net a hundred bucks after taxes and paying my agent."

Heather blinked multiple times before she realized she must look like Dora Chen. "You have an agent?"

Steve lifted another bite of pie. "Kate's my agent and writing coach."

"I thought she was your editor."

He spoke around the next bite of pecan pie. "She is."

While sitting in stunned silence, a revelation hit Heather. She stared at him. "You waited for the perfect time to tell me this, didn't you? I'm used to playing this game in making business deals, but not in murder investigations."

"What game?"

"Don't give me the innocent act. You didn't tell me you knew Detective Hall and I had copies of Melody's tax returns, knowing I'd get mad at myself for not figuring it out. Now, your relationship with Kate is back to where it was before we solved the murder of her ex-husband. I bet if I think about it long enough, I'll see you left me hints about that, too."

Steve issued what she called his little boy smile, the one that telegraphed naughty and lovable at the same time. He added melodramatic words to his smile. "My world is dark, small, and boring. Sparring with you, the occasional case, and writing are all I have to keep me from going mad."

Heather struck back with sarcasm as she took her napkin and attacked the coffee she'd spilled. "I'll call Kate and congratulate her on shaping you into the next Hemmingway."

Steve's eyebrows rose above his dark glasses. "Are you sure you don't want a piece of pie to celebrate?"

"I'll celebrate when you sell a novel." He'd won the skirmish, but she looked forward to the next battle of wits.

With appetites appeased, the two made their way home in silence. Heather took one bag of leftovers into Steve's condo while he carried the other. Her phone came alive as she moved things around in the refrigerator. She considered not answering it until she saw her father's name on the caller ID.

Her voice crackled with a tense, "Hello, Father."

He mumbled something and cleared his throat. When he spoke, it came out in a hoarse whisper. "Heather, you need to come home. It's your mother."

Time stopped. "What's wrong with Mother?"

A long pause followed. "She died this morning."

15

———

Steve walked into the kitchen. "Did I hear your phone ring?"
Silence filled the room.

"Heather? Are you alright?"

"I need to get to Boston."

"Is something wrong?"

"Mother—" Her voice cracked and she tried again. "Mother died... this morning."

He answered in a soft, calming tone. "Oh. I'm so sorry, Heather." The hum of the refrigerator told him she still held the door open. The condiments rattled when she closed it. Steve held up his hand. "I know your first instinct is to take off at a run, but slow down and get paper and a pen. The notepad by the toaster will do. We'll make a plan that will save you time."

Seconds later, she stood at the counter with pen and paper in hand. "I need to call Jack."

"Why don't we go sit down? You need a lot of things, and if you rush, you'll forget something important. Calling Jack will be the first thing on your list."

"What do you mean, *my list?*"

"Let's sit down and I'll tell you."

The sound of Heather's slacks sliding on the fabric of a dining room chair reached Steve's ears. He continued to speak in a tone he hoped would combine sympathy with business. "Draw a line down the center of the pad. Write your name at the top of the left column and put mine over the right."

The sound of pen on paper ceased. "What's next?"

"In my column, write, *Call Pilots.* Next, in my column again, write something to the effect that I'll call your personal assistant at work."

"I should do that."

Steve lowered his voice. "You can give her a follow-up call from the car or your airplane if you need to." He moved on so she wouldn't get bogged down with details. "How are you set for clean clothes? You'll need several things in black. Plan on being gone for a week."

"I'm in good shape, but it wouldn't hurt if I had a new dress."

"I'll tell your PA to make several selections and have them delivered to your father's home."

He waited until she asked, "What's next?"

"Do you have cash?"

"Not much, but plenty of credit cards."

"I keep a stash of bills in my sock drawer. I'll get it for you while you pack."

"That's unnecessary. I can—"

"I know you can, but this is one time when you need to allow others to help you."

The sharp exhale of air meant she'd agreed. He pushed back from the table but didn't stand.

"Is that all?"

"When you call Jack, tell him to pick you up here."

"You didn't say 'us.'"

Steve stood. "I'm not going. The one thing you don't need is to show up with two men, and one of them blind. You'll have enough tongues wagging when you walk in with a handsome

Texas attorney on your arm. My being there would mean too many questions to answer, and your mother's wake and funeral aren't the place to explain that you work with a blind ex-cop."

He sensed she'd say something to contradict him, so he played his ace in the hole. "Besides, I need to stay here and work on the case. You can stay in touch with me by phone and emails. If you're wondering how I'll get around, I already have that covered."

"Uber?"

"Don't worry about me. I manage when you're at work every day." What she didn't know was he'd already come up with a different and much better plan than Uber.

"Now, you'd better get started packing."

"I don't like the idea of leaving you here alone," said Heather.

"I'm never here alone. Max doesn't say much, but he's a skilled listener."

Heather took a step, stopped, then moved toward him. Steve found himself enveloped in her arms and reciprocated with a firm hug as her body shook. Sobs flowed. He held on until she released her grip.

"One last thing," said Steve. "Take a nice, long shower after you call Jack. What came over you just now will come and go in waves. Crying in the shower helps get it out and cleans up the mess at the same time."

Doors opened and closed. He heard Heather speaking through the kitty door. Her conversation with Jack lasted longer than he thought it would. The conveyance of information came out slowly, delayed by grief-filled pauses. With no siblings and only a handful of distant relatives, she'd never experienced the loss of an immediate family member.

He went to his chair in the living room, placed the first call to Heather's pilot and informed him to do everything necessary to get Heather and Jack to Boston tonight. Although she believed in and practiced meticulous planning, spur-of-the-moment flights popped up from time to time. The pilot and copilot had instructions to have their go-bags packed and ready at a moment's notice.

Next, he called Heather's personal assistant, a woman of remarkable composure and efficiency. She was two steps ahead of him concerning Heather's clothing needs and suggested a tasteful black hat with a short veil, as the funeral would likely be a high church affair.

Steve went to his sock drawer and pulled out five hundred dollars in fifties, twenties, and tens. Heather never tipped less than ten dollars. He heard water running in the pipes in the wall that separated Heather's bathroom from his.

Back in the living room, he informed Max of the death of Heather's mother, and that she would be gone for many days. The cat responded by slipping his head under Steve's hand and then padding to the pet portal. The sound of the plastic flapping shut confirmed he'd gone to check on her.

Steve then raised his phone, took in a deep breath, and spoke into it. "Call Kate."

The phone rang six times before it went to voice mail. While listening to the rings, he remembered the time and realized she worked without interruption from after lunch until five. The electronic beep prompted him to leave a message.

"Kate, it's Steve. Please call. I need help."

"Good," he whispered to himself. "That gives me time to make necessary arrangements."

STEVE SAT IN A WINGBACK CHAIR IN HEATHER'S LIVING ROOM, listening to her pace back and forth. He lifted his chin when he heard a car door slam. "There's Jack; his door makes a very distinct sound. He'll soon have his bags and hanging clothes in your SUV. We might as well say goodbye now."

"I still don't feel right about leaving you here alone in the middle of a case. Are you sure Leo can't help you while I'm gone?"

"I wouldn't dare ask him this time. He leaves tomorrow on the big family vacation he's saved years for. I'm not sure if his wife would kill him, me, or both of us if he canceled at the last minute."

"That's right. I remember you telling me about his big trip to Yellowstone." Heather took in a breath. "Thanks for the cash. That will save us a stop."

Once again, Steve found himself in Heather's arms. The hug came without tears and ended with a promise to call when they landed safely in Boston.

"Don't worry about things here. Take care of your father. He'll need you."

The next thing Steve heard was Heather groan a little and say, "Max. You be a good boy and take care of Steve."

Cat claws made soft clicks as Heather lowered her tubby cat to the tile floor. Footsteps tracked to the door, and the knob made a click when she turned it. The sound of humming air conditioners and street noises filtered in and went away as soon as Heather closed the door behind her. Steve spoke to Max. "It's me and you tonight, and she didn't tell me I couldn't spoil you. How 'bout we have fried catfish?"

Steve moved to the door. "I'll meet you on the other side of your kitty door. Kate should call before long."

The phone rang before Steve sat in his recliner. Kate's first words came out colored with concern. "What's wrong? Are you alright?"

"I'm fine. It's Heather's mother. She died this morning."

A gasp and a moan preceded Kate's next sentences. "I'm so sorry. I suppose you called to tell me you're heading to Boston with her."

"She and Jack are on their way. I'm staying here."

"Ah, I understand. How does that make you feel?"

"The closest thing I can think of is the way a parent must feel when their child goes off to college. On the one hand, I'm sad things are changing, but on the other hand, I'm happy they are. It's the natural order of things."

A brief pause followed. "Is their relationship that serious?"

"It could be if she'd stop trying to prove herself. She comes from such extreme wealth that she thinks if she doesn't leave a bigger pile of it when she dies, she's a failure."

"Have you ever talked to her about it?"

"Not directly, but I suggested she buy a catamaran so she and Jack could sail to Belize, check on her project down there, then enjoy herself, and Jack, for a few days. If she would allow herself to get away from her focus of building more wealth, she might be able to see what she's in danger of missing. Her Midas touch with investments is holding her back from a commitment. In some ways, she's a victim of success."

"That's a very unique problem." Kate took in a deep breath. "What about her partnership with you? Do you sense that's ending, too?"

"That's different. We only work on three or four cases a year and they always refresh her. With Jack being a defense attorney, it gives them common ground. He's good at giving her a different perspective, which everyone needs."

"Now you're stepping on my toes," said Kate with levity creeping into her voice. "I'm having a hard time with that short story idea you gave me. I'm so used to writing historical romance novels that getting the feel of what it's like to deal with a modern crime is stretching my mind."

Steve chuckled. "Funny you should mention that. It seems I'm short an assistant and could use someone with your unique qualifications."

Kate's levity morphed into a full-blown laugh. Once she controlled the residual giggles, she said, "I don't believe writing novels involving pretend romances in Elizabethan England qualifies me for dealing with actual crimes."

"You've already helped me with two previous cases. Besides, there are two things that make you more than qualified for what I need."

"I'm listening, but I'm having a hard time believing what you're saying."

How could he seal the deal? Then he remembered the words he'd spoken to Detective Hall. *Tell the truth.* Good advice, but he couldn't put on too much pressure. He took in a deep breath. "First, as an editor, you find flaws in logic and timing. You also give fantastic descriptions of people and places. I can see the pictures you paint with words."

"Thanks for the flattery, but it will take more than that to get me to help you after what happened last time."

Steve had to come up with something fast or his plan would sink like an anvil in a lake. It came to him in a flash. "Your writing improved after you got out and experienced life."

"Life? It felt more like imminent death."

"You were never in any real danger. Heather and I saw to that."

"True, but you forgot to let me in on that minor point."

Steve allowed several seconds of silence to pass before Kate's voice came again. "I hate to admit you're right, but the novel I wrote after that ordeal on South Padre Island is my best seller ever."

Steve nodded in self-satisfaction. He almost had her, but needed one more push. "There's one other thing you possess that makes you qualified to help me."

"What's that?"

"You have a driver's license."

Her laughter came in waves.

Once he could get in a word, he added details. "You're scheduled for a 9:00 a.m. flight out of Miami tomorrow morning. I've reserved a rental car for you at Houston's airport. An email with all the information is on its way, and Heather has a spare bedroom ready for you."

"You're quite the salesman, Detective Smiley."

"I'll bring you up to speed on the case tomorrow afternoon, and if there's time, we'll go back to the crime scene."

16

Heather and Jack settled on a couch in the library of the house she grew up in. The morning had gone by at a snail's pace. She could only imagine how boring it must be for Jack to come to a home that always seemed so lifeless. Like walking into a museum, but without patrons and groups of visitors.

Steve was right about there being no need for her to rush. Her father operated under the firm belief that if you had enough money to hire people, then you simply told them what to do. This left time to devote yourself to more useful pursuits. To Father, that meant continue to grow the family fortune. When something like the unexpected death of a spouse broke into his routine, it left him at loose ends, not knowing what to do in the period between death and burial. His *people* took care of the arrangements, leaving Heather and her father with empty blocks of time. Nothing to do but consume meals three times a day, and grieve.

The priest, a man with compassionate brown eyes and a fringe of white hair, had spoken all the right words to her the previous night and promised to return with a draft of the funeral service for approval. Household staff went about their duties with extra care to remain unseen as much as possible. The mood seemed as dark as the stained bookcases in the room where Heather sat holding Jack's hand.

"This is torture," said Heather in a whisper, even though she'd closed the door behind them for privacy.

"You and your father are so much alike. It drives both of you nuts if you're not wheeling and dealing. He's in the study walking a hole in the carpet, and you and I are in here."

"He said he wanted to be alone."

Jack's eyebrows rose as she continued. "I think he'd rather be in his office at McBlythe Enterprises, pulling off another deal, but propriety constrains him to stay home until after the funeral."

Jack shook his head. "He'll never make it that long, and I'm not sure you will either. We need to get him out."

Heather tilted her head. "Out where?"

"Out of this mausoleum and into the sunshine."

"That doesn't seem right so soon after Mother died."

Jack turned toward her. "I didn't say today, but it's four more days before the funeral and burial. Let me ask him to show us around Boston. I flew in for a baseball game once, but Fenway Park is all I ever saw." He paused. "Tell me, wouldn't you rather show me all your old hangouts than sit in this room? He's experiencing the same thing you are."

She wagged her head. "I don't think he'll go, but it's worth a shot. I know I'll be easier to live with if we can do something besides stare at old books."

Jack leaned over and gave her a kiss on the cheek. "That's my girl. Even if he turns me down, let's sneak out and take a walk tonight."

Heather couldn't help but grin. "That brings back memories. I used to do that when I'd come home from boarding school. The staff had to have known what I was up to."

"They didn't tell your parents?"

"If they did, Father and Mother said nothing about it.

There's a rule in polite society that you can do just about anything as long as you keep your name out of the newspapers and your face off television... unless, of course, it's for a charity event."

Jack released her hand. "Wish me luck."

"You'll need more than luck. He's used to negotiating deals. Ask him to go out with us for three days and you'll be lucky to get him to agree to one."

Jack gave her a wink. "He'll be putty in my hands."

"In your dreams."

Heather watched until the door shut behind the man who'd made significant inroads into her heart. She pondered the situation she found herself in and wondered if Jack's presence resulted from her desire for him to be at her side, Steve's manipulation, or both. She decided it didn't matter and removed her phone from the mahogany table crowned by a Tiffany lamp.

Steve answered on the second ring. "I didn't expect to hear from you so soon. How's your father holding up?"

"He's so stoic it's hard to tell. I'm sure he grieved in private before we arrived last night, and he looked like he hadn't slept at all when he came to breakfast."

"Did he pick you up at the airport?"

"He sent the chauffeur."

"Is he eating?"

"Nothing for breakfast, and he didn't read his newspaper. He had a few bites of lunch and went to his office. Jack's with him now, trying to talk him into a tour of Boston."

"That would be the best thing for everyone. What are Jack's chances of success?"

"Normally I'd say zero, but Jack has a subtle way of getting to people. Even if Father doesn't go, Jack suggested we sneak out tonight. I need a break from all this doom and gloom."

"Did you have another good cry on the airplane?"

"I ruined my makeup and had to reapply it before we landed.

Sleep evaded me most of the night, but I think the worst is over."

"Remember," said Steve. "It comes in waves. Keep tissues handy. The funeral service may not be for days, but expect some waterworks when you're there, and at graveside."

Heather wanted to move on and talk about something besides her mother's death, but didn't want to appear hardhearted. Steve saved her from guilt by changing subjects. "I made arrangements to talk to Cindy Green this evening. I want to find out how upset she was, and possibly still is, about not getting the sales manager's position."

"Jack and I had a brief conversation on the plane about motive. We concluded there's something we're not seeing. Cindy not getting promoted seems like a weak reason to steal tax information."

"Not necessarily. Something's been niggling my brain about those records. If I get a handle on what it is, I'll have you and Jack do a little research while you're sitting around with nothing to do but stare at the walls."

Heather wanted to ask how he knew so much about her day's activities, but wrote it off to Steve's sixth sense... or was it telepathy he used? No matter.

"One more thing, Heather. Is it all right if Kate uses your spare bedroom?"

"Kate? She's coming to see you?"

"I needed a driver, and she's having trouble writing a short story in a genre that's not her strength."

"She isn't allergic to cats, is she?"

"She knows Max has free run of both condos."

"Kate can come any time and stay as long as she likes." Heather paused, then dug deeper. "Are you looking for someone to replace me?"

The response came back quick. Perhaps too fast, like Steve might have practiced it.

"Absolutely not. Not only can you drive me wherever I need

to go, you have several very nice pistols, a P.I. license, a license to practice law, a posh private jet, and you're a former detective who knows what questions to ask. All Kate can do is drive and write stories. You're stuck with me."

"I think it's you who's stuck with me," said Heather through a small lump in her throat.

"Good. Now that we have that settled, expect an enormous expense on my company credit card. I flew Kate first class to Houston today and rented her a luxury car to drive. She should be here any time."

"We'll bill our client for it," said Heather.

"Do you think Chris has enough money to pay the bill?"

"That's a question for another day."

"Tell Jack I said hello."

"Let me know if you determine what's niggling you about motive, and tell Kate to make herself at home." She spoke up as something else popped into her mind. "And no more letting Max eat off your plate."

"I wouldn't dream of it."

Heather couldn't contain the smile. "That means you and Max had something special last night. What was it?"

"Catfish. He insisted."

Steve moved on before she could reprimand him. "I think I heard a car door. Call tomorrow and I'll give you an update."

KATE DIDN'T ARRIVE FOR ANOTHER HOUR. STEVE MET HER outside Heather's door, unsure of how warm a reception to give or what to expect. The answer came when she gave him a peck on the cheek. He thought it a suitable compromise between her grabbing an awkward hand thrust into space and a more intimate hug. The light scent of her perfume brought back memories of being with her. She hadn't switched to something more overpowering, which pleased him.

"You're looking fit," said Kate. "Spending time on the treadmill?"

"Not as much as I need to. Let's get inside before this heat melts both of us." He punched a series of buttons on Heather's lock, heard the door click, and pushed it open. "I'll send you a text with the code. How many suitcases?"

"Two, and a backpack with my computer and the rest of my traveling office. I'll roll the first one to you and you can lead the way to my room."

"It's easy to find. The first door on the right past the living room. The guest bathroom is across the hall."

"Where's Max?"

"On the couch when I left my condo. He'll make his grand entrance after he yawns, stretches, and takes a cat bath. If you don't want him in bed with you tonight, you'll need to shut your door."

"This is his house. If he can stand me, I'd love to have a furry bed partner."

Steve rolled the first suitcase into the spare bedroom and hoisted it onto the queen size bed. "Do you need help with the second one?"

"I gave you the heaviest of the two. This room is perfect."

Steve nodded. "The condo has a simple layout. Explore. There are drinks, fresh fruit and yogurt in the refrigerator. Everything in the freezer and pantry in both condos is fair game. Did they feed you on the plane?"

"You set the bar high by getting me a first-class seat. The meal exceeded my expectations. I may not need to eat tonight."

Steve took a step toward the bedroom door. "Thanks so much for coming."

Her hand rested on his arm. "Thank you for asking. I can't believe this is our third adventure together. I hope Heather doesn't think I'm trying to take her place."

"She called today, and we talked about that very thing. I hope this doesn't come out wrong, but she'll always be the first person I call to help solve a murder."

Kate gave her trademark laugh that sounded like joy spilling out of a bottle. "I can't even drive as good as she can."

"Few people can. She took extra lessons from a Formula One driver after her police training." Steve paused. "I'll let you get freshened up. Come next door whenever you're ready. We have plenty of time before we talk to a person of interest this evening."

"How exciting. A person of interest."

"That's the plan. Her name is Cindy Green. I believe she could be a disgruntled employee, but I want to find out for sure."

The sound of the kitty door flapping shut reached Steve's ears. "Here's Max. I hope you're ready for him."

Steve made it almost to the front door when Kate gushed a greeting to Heather's spoiled child. "My goodness. If you're not the most lovable thing I've ever seen. Come to the bedroom, help me unpack, and I'll tell you a story. It's about a little girl and her kitty who grew up together in a manor house in England."

Steve closed the front door behind him. Max had found his next bed buddy.

With that out of the way, he went to his recliner and mentally sifted through the suspects. One was the woman they'd see in a couple of hours, Cindy Green.

17

S teve heard the knock on the front door as the pet portal slapped shut at the same time. "It's unlocked." He knew it was Kate by the sound of her approaching footsteps. "Max took a shortcut and beat you here."

"Don't call the police if he goes missing on the same day I go back to Miami. He'll be having the time of his life playing in the sand and eating fresh seafood."

Steve held up both hands. "Leave me out of any cat-napping scheme you're planning. Remember, he's Heather's only child, so you might have a fight on your hands." He changed the tone of his voice to something more contemplative. "She's not hard-wired for a human child."

"She still has plenty of time," said Kate as she sat on the couch within touching distance.

Steve shook his head. "I don't think maternal instinct made it into either of her double helix strands of DNA."

Kate chucked. "I'm definitely stealing that line for a future book. I can already picture a beautiful but flighty ingenue who makes babies cry and young children scream if she gets within five feet of them."

Steve turned his head. "How do you do that?"

"Do what?"

"Find characters, plots, and conflict in so many of the things I say?"

She stayed silent for a few seconds before she spoke in a softer tone. "You don't realize how unique you are, and it's not because you lost your sight."

"Unique. I'm not sure if that's a compliment or a complaint."

"It's certainly good for my writing. Perhaps I should pay you by the word for all the things I'm stealing from you."

"You'll need to speak to my agent about that."

"I would, but I'd have to talk to myself. I've heard a person can be put away for that type of thing."

Steve smiled and scratched his chin. "There's a lot about the book business I still need to learn."

Kate stood. "And speaking of the book business. I need to spend a couple of hours at the dining room table answering emails and writing a blog for my readers. Wait until they read that I'm on a last-minute trip to work with a real private detective."

"Please tell me you don't use my name."

"All names and locations are fictitious. It cuts down on lawsuits." She took a breath. "Is there coffee?"

Steve placed his hands on the arms of his recliner and pushed himself to a standing position. "Set up your workspace and I'll make coffee. Then, I'll leave you to it. If you hear snoring, ignore it."

He meant the line about snoring to be a joke, but awakened two hours later to Kate's light tap on his bedroom door. He acknowledged her and said he'd be ready to leave in five minutes. While brushing his teeth, he pondered why he'd tossed and turned most of last night. He wrote it off to his undependable circadian rhythm. Most sighted people had the sun to tell them when to rise and prepare for bed. On most days, he slept when he grew tired, no matter the time of day.

Once in the rental, Steve clicked his seat belt in place. "Nice leather. I can tell by the height this isn't an SUV. What did I rent for you?"

"It's a Volvo SC60 with seventy-two miles on it."

He nodded his approval. "It smells new."

"I'm not used to such luxury. Discount airlines and small hybrid rentals are more my style."

"Mine too, but I thought I needed to put some good bait on the hook to get you to come. Besides, I already told Heather the plane tickets and this ride will be a business expense."

Kate waited a minute before she asked, "What's it like working with someone who has endless financial resources?"

Steve thought back several years. "You should have known her when we first met. Heather barely had enough money to keep Max in cat food. In fact, I gave her room, board, and spending money to help me solve our first murder case. Her father hated her decision to become a cop in Boston and did everything he could to make her life miserable. He had enough pull to have her fired. One of her grandparents, the maternal grandfather, left her a ton of money in his will, but she couldn't get to it until she turned thirty. When I met her, her father was hot on her trail again and she needed to hide out a few weeks until she came into her inheritance. Since then, she's been obsessed with growing that fortune."

The blinker of the car made its unique clicking sound. "We're pulling into the parking lot," said Kate before she returned to the subject. "All that is great backstory information, but you didn't answer my question. What's it like working and living with someone with millions to spare?"

"Hundreds of millions to spare," said Steve. "In fact, her wealth may soon double. Her parents kept their family fortunes mostly separate when they married. It's likely Heather's mother left most everything to her."

"Wow."

Steve heard and felt the car come to a complete stop and the transmission go into park. "To answer your question, let's just say

Heather doesn't look for sales in the grocery store and allows her personal assistant to pick out her clothes. Yet, she lives in a two-bedroom condo and drops everything when we find a murder that needs solving."

"Are you saying she moves effortlessly between the two worlds?"

Steve reached for the door handle. "Yeah. Pretty cool, huh?"

"Astounding."

Steve changed his tone. "Do you remember the name of the woman we're here to talk to?"

"Cindy Green."

"Right. I'll do most of the talking, but jump in if a question rises to the surface."

The passenger side door closed with a deep thunk, the sound of quality engineering and a tight fit. Kate's door made the same sound. He unfurled his cane, found the curb, and stepped onto a sidewalk. Kate met him at the front of the Volvo, placed his hand on her arm, and they made their way to Melody Craddock's eyeglass store.

Once inside the door, Kate stopped. "Let me take off my sunglasses and put them in my purse."

"Do you wear glasses all the time?" asked Steve.

"Only when I'm working on the computer."

Steve chuckled. "That would be most of the day."

"Not as much as years past. I'm learning to pace myself. My goal is to write three hours in the morning and devote my afternoons to business."

"What about the evenings?"

"Relax and do whatever I want. I watch a lot of British television."

"You didn't mention swimming. Are you still doing laps?"

"Every morning. I cut my hair to make it easier to dry."

She took his hand and raised it, allowing Steve to run it down the back of her head. Her hair ended where the collar of her blouse began.

"It's thick, soft, and has plenty of waves," said Steve.

"You'll need to thank my hairdresser for the extra volume, the result of a perm."

Steve pulled his hand down. "Every time I hear the word perm, I get the mental image of a standard poodle in need of a dog groomer."

Her laugh spilled out again. "There's another line I'll need to jot down. You'll have that first-class ticket paid for in no time."

The sound of at least two people passing them caused Steve to take a step to the side. He waited until the door shut. "How many customers are in the store?"

"No one is standing except one bored looking man wearing a hat with a golf logo on it. There're three employees at various tables with as many customers."

"Pretend you're looking for glasses."

"Who's pretending? I ran off and left mine in Miami."

Steve squared his shoulders. "How are you able to work?"

"I can pick up some cheap magnifiers at any drug store. They'll work until I get home." Kate then whispered. "A clerk is coming this way."

Steve whispered back, "Is it Cindy?"

"Can I help you?"

Steve remained silent, not knowing if this was Cindy or another employee.

"Thanks, but we need to speak with Cindy," said Kate.

"I'll let her know you're waiting."

Steve stood silent, leaning on his cane, until Kate whispered, "The salesperson turned off the open sign and walked to the back."

Kate kept Steve informed as, in quick succession, all remaining customers and sales clerks left the building, except one.

"Sorry to keep you waiting. I'll be glad to stay and help you but... Oh my gosh, it can't be. Stay here while I get something. I'll be right back. Don't move!"

Running footfalls headed away from where Steve and Kate stood. "Why did she run away?" asked Steve.

Kate chuckled. "I think you're about to meet what's called a super-fan of historical romance novels."

Footfalls came back and stopped in front of Kate. "I can't believe it. Kate Bridges is standing in front of me." Her sentences ran together like watercolors. "I thought you lived in Miami. Please tell me you moved to Texas. Look. I have your latest book, *A KNIGHT TO FORGET*. My heart stopped when Sir Cedric pushed Lady Penelope off the cliff. Little did he know the Earl of Newberry had placed a hidden rope in the exact spot where she would stand when the evil knight gave her a shove."

Cindy finally took a breath. "I knew she was a goner, but true love triumphed again. Please sign my book."

"Of course. Let's have a seat at one of these tables."

After Kate took care of personalizing the inscription and signing her name, she made introductions. "This is a dear friend of mine, Steve Smiley."

Steve gave Cindy a nod and a quick, "Nice to meet you. I'm a private investigator looking into the death of Cleo Stanley. My regular partner has already been here and interviewed Bryson Wayne. Unfortunately, Ms. McBlythe is out of state, so I called Kate to help me."

Kate spoke next. "Besides being an investigator, Steve is also an up-and-coming writer and a great inspiration for many things that appear in my books."

Steve imagined Cindy sitting on the edge of her seat, wide-eyed and staring at Kate.

"Wow. I can't believe I'm talking to Kate Bridges."

Steve cleared his throat. "So, did you know Cleo well?"

"Oh, sorry. I didn't mean to carry on so, but I've never met a famous author." She cleared her throat. "I didn't know Cleo well. I got to know her when she first started cleaning the practice and retail store. Then her company added more and more businesses for her to clean. This became her last stop of the night, because it's the easiest to clean. Eyeglass stores don't get too dirty, but they need to be as spotless as possible to make a good impression."

Steve continued. "Do you get along with the other employees here?"

"Yeah. It's a good crew. I helped Dr. Melody open the store before she went back to college and became an optometrist. I had a hand in hiring many of the sales clerks."

"Did you resent it when Melody chose Bryson Wayne to manage this store?"

"Yes, but I got over it. Looking back, Bryson's such a high energy guy and a stickler for details. I don't blame him or Dr. Melody."

Kate broke in. "That's very magnanimous of you."

A laugh trickled out of Cindy. "I had to look that word up when I read your novel, *NO MANNERS IN THE MANOR*. I loved it when Roxanne, the scullery maid, who was really a French aristocrat, took the rough edges off the Marquess of Midbourne after his release from a Spanish prison where Count Flambeau held him for ransom most of his life."

Cindy took a gasping breath to replenish all she'd expelled.

Steve turned to Kate. "You ask the next question. My head's spinning."

Kate must have covered the chuckle with her hand as it came out muffled. "Isn't Steve a delightful kidder?"

"I think he's cute."

"Me, too," said Kate in a fake whisper. He wondered if she threw in a wink for good measure.

Steve took over. "It's our understanding that whoever was here took some records from the back office. Do you know what those were?"

"I looked in the file after the police finished and took down all the yellow tape. They were the tax records for both businesses."

Steve nodded, if for no other reason than to reinforce her answer. "Why would someone want to steal those?"

"I gave that plenty of thought and couldn't think of a good reason." Cindy paused, "Unless..."

"Yes?" said Kate.

"I didn't think of it before, but in one of your first novels, *MY HEART FOR A RANSOM*, an emissary from Portugal approaches Lord Ashley who wants to know if the full amount of silver for a trade deal is being loaded onto one ship or two."

"I don't understand what that has to do with tax returns," said Kate.

Steve stood. "Thanks for your time, Cindy. You've given me something to think about." He sat back down. "There may be one more thing you can help us with before we go, but first I'll need Kate to answer one question."

"Me?"

"When was your last eye exam?"

She let out another of her laughs, followed by, "You sounded so serious."

"I am."

Still laughing, she said, "I don't know. Two, no, three years ago."

"Cindy, can you cut through the red tape for us and see if you can get Kate in to see Dr. Melody sometime tomorrow?"

"Most employees don't know it, but our system can interface with the one next door. Let me look at Dr. Melody's schedule."

Keys clicked on a computer keyboard. After a few Ums and Ahs, Melody spoke with confidence. "She has a full day, but there's a nine o'clock open. Probably a last-minute cancellation that wasn't filled. Will that work?"

"Perfect," said Steve. "How long does it take to get glasses delivered?"

"I can put a rush on and they'll be here overnight if it's not a complicated prescription."

"Do you have time tonight for Kate to pick out frames?"

"Are you kidding? I'd stay here until dawn for Kate Bridges."

The mood in the car going home was buoyant until Kate said, "Cindy said something that clicked with you. What was it?"

"I need to run it by Heather first. It's a long shot, but it might be what we've been looking for."

"You can't tell me tonight?"

"We're going out to eat and talk about anything but the case."

Kate grumbled. "Now I know how my readers feel when I write cliffhangers."

18

———

The alarm on Steve's phone roused him from a nonsensical dream where he and Heather raced against each other in matching Formula One cars. He blamed the dream on last night's lasagna with Kate. Then he realized his first thoughts of the day didn't include his late wife, Maggie. A wave of guilt flowed and then ebbed away as soon as his toes dug into the carpet by his bed.

He arrived in the kitchen and went about making coffee. Max let out a loud meow, his way of ordering breakfast. It wasn't long before sounds of life filtered through the walls. Steve sat at the table when Kate pushed open the plastic flap separating the two condos. "Is that coffee I smell?"

"It's ready when you are."

"Pour me a cup."

In less than a minute, they sat on opposite sides of the table, content to remain silent until the stimulant worked its magic. He'd noticed before, and appreciated, how Kate eased into her day. So unlike Heather who wanted her mind stimulated with the latest news from the overseas markets as soon as possible. He could only imagine how bored she was in Boston, waiting for a funeral.

Kate broke her silence when he rose to refill his mug. "Did you call Heather last night?"

"I'm giving her a little more time. I want to talk again with Dr. Melody and her assistant, Dora Chen. After that, I'll call Heather and give her a couple of things to do."

"Do you think she'll be up to it? I mean, won't she be grieving or helping her father with the funeral?"

Steve didn't know exactly how to explain the McBlythe family dynamics, but he'd do his best and hope Kate understood. "From what I've learned over the years, the McBlythes are not like the rest of us. Heather comes from a bloodline of people who don't show emotion in public. Heather's different. More human, but sometimes she relapses into old ways. Jack picked her up after she had a good cry with me. She trusts Jack, and had another good cry on the airplane. She might have a tear or two left for the funeral, but I think that's all the grieving she'll do for her mother."

"You make her sound hard-hearted."

"They trained her not to display emotions. Emotionally, her father's an iceberg, and her mother wasn't much better. They loved Heather in their own way, but that included contracting with others to display love and affection. Heather received small portions of affection, maybe even a form of love, from nannies, tutors, and teachers at boarding schools. She lacked for nothing except what people long for the most. Not much love grows in the rarefied air of the ultra-rich."

"Is she an ice queen?"

"She would have been if she hadn't rebelled and become a cop. Making it in Boston on just a cop's salary put a good dose of humility and human suffering in her."

The sound of Kate taking a quick sip of coffee and the mug coming to rest again on the table made it to Steve's ears. So did Kate's next words. "You love her dearly, don't you?"

"I imagine her sometimes as my baby sister, who someone kidnapped as a child and she grew up as a princess."

"That explains a lot, but not why you didn't check on her last night."

How could Steve put this in a way that made sense? He'd have to trust Kate to read between the lines. "This trip to Boston is a watershed moment for Heather. She's going to face the biggest decision of her life, and I want to give her every chance to live the rest of her life without a huge regret."

"It sounds like you believe you know what's best for her."

"I think I do, but in the end, that won't matter. It will be her choice and I'll support her either way."

"And what is this make-or-break decision?"

"I'm surprised you haven't already figured it out."

"I see that smirk pulling the corner of your mouth, Detective Smiley. You're playing the same game with Heather's choice that you did last night by not telling me what you discovered while talking to Cindy Green. Now you've left me hanging over a pit, worried about Heather."

Steve pushed back from the table. "How do you want your eggs this morning?"

"I'd like them raw and poured over your head."

He moved to the refrigerator and withdrew a carton of eggs. "I specialize in undercooked food, so if you want a decent breakfast, you'd better give me a hand." He took a quick breath. "I've been listening to podcasts about artificial intelligence voice narration for audio books. What's your opinion?"

"My opinion on AI narration is that you changed the subject and I may double your order of raw eggs."

Kate's laugh bounced off every hard surface in the kitchen. The more he heard her laugh, the more he liked it. Not as good as Maggie's laugh, but good in a different way.

STEVE AND KATE ARRIVED FOR HER APPOINTMENT AT DR. Melody's office ten minutes early. He sat in a chair that felt surprisingly familiar. Then it occurred to him, it was identical to the one he'd sat in at Dr. Chris's waiting room. In fact, the acoustics were the same, as was the placement of the receptionist. Chris had made a carbon copy of his previous workplace.

The sound of a door opening caught his attention and Dora Chen's distinct voice announced, "Kate Bridges? Ms. Kate Bridges, please follow me."

Steve stood and Kate placed his hand on her arm. The door closed behind them and Dora said, "Ah, Mr. Smiley. You must have misunderstood me. I called for Ms. Bridges. If you're here to see Dr. Craddock, you'll need to wait."

Kate spoke up. "Mr. Smiley is with me today."

Steve took over. "We do need to talk to Dr. Melody, but first I need to clarify some things you said the other day."

"Only patients in treatment rooms."

Kate spoke up. "I saw a husband and wife come in together, and don't parents accompany their children during exams?"

"Are you husband and wife?"

"No."

"Then it's not permitted."

Steve raised his cane to an upright position. "We thought it would save time if you answered my questions while you checked Kate's eyes. Otherwise, I'll have to speak with Melody. She'll tell you to talk to me, which I'll do in the presence of Ms. Bridges. The outcome will be the same, but you'll get behind in your duties."

Her accent grew thicker and her tone more defiant. "I don't have to talk to you."

"That's true, but then I'd have to call Detective Hall. He'd insist on interviewing you and would allow me to be present." Steve paused. "If you think it's worth missing half a day of work to go to Detective Hall's office, that's fine with me."

After a huff and something muttered in a foreign language, Dora said, "You can come along, but my work is more important than your questions."

Dora closed the treatment room door behind them and took control. "Ms. Bridges, have a seat in the exam chair. Mr. Smiley, you must stand out of the way. To save time, don't talk to me until I'm through with the refraction and administer the dilation drops."

Steve heard Dora sit in a rolling chair and the sound of a computer terminal coming to life. The optometrist's assistant then peppered Kate with demographic and medical questions. Kate answered them just as fast. Before long, Dora said. "Use this to cover the left eye. What's the smallest line you can read?" Then Dora gave instructions about the machine Kate was to look through and they played the game of, "Which looks better, this one, or this one?" Metallic clicks of lenses shifting into place accompanied Kate's quick, sure responses.

Dora then said, "Lean your head back. Only one drop in each eye for dilation. Normally we use two, but your eyes are healthy. Use this tissue to dab away any excess, but don't scratch your eye."

The sound of the roller chair being put back in its place caught Steve attention. "Now, Mr. Smiley, you have four minutes to ask your questions."

"It probably won't take that long. Does Dr. Melody know you were an optometrist in South Korea?"

"How did you find out?" demanded Dora.

"I didn't know for sure until now. As you can imagine, I have a better than average knowledge of the eye and its workings. Or in my case, how the eyes no longer work. You gave yourself away with some of the questions you asked Kate, and exceeded your authority by concluding Kate has healthy eyes."

"Will you tell Dr. Melody?"

"Not if you answer the rest of my questions."

She hesitated. "Ask, but I think you're a bad person for tricking me."

Steve ignored the hostility. "Did you steal the documents from the file cabinet in the business next door?"

"No."

"Do you have any idea who did?"

"Why don't you ask the manager?"

"I'm asking you."

"I don't like to speculate. Ask the store's manager or Dr. Melody."

"Are you aware of another optometrist or ophthalmologist who might want to take over this practice?"

"No."

"What about a business person?"

"Why would someone like that want to take over an optometrist's practice?"

"Don't play like you don't already know. Big corporations take over successful businesses all the time, including optometrists' practices. Are you aware of anyone talking to Dr. Melody about selling her practice and the store next door?"

"I do my work and go home. The only people I pay attention to are my patients. Your four minutes are up." The door opened. "Ms. Bridges, Dr. Melody will be in to see you soon. She'll complete the exam and give you a prescription."

The door closed with more force than necessary. Kate issued a loud whisper. "I'm impressed. You tricked her into admitting she was an optometrist in South Korea."

"I sometimes stretch the truth during interviews. All that stuff about my knowledge of the eye and how she gave herself away by her exam procedures was a shot in the dark. It's part of the game of verifying what I know to be true and pushing enough buttons to see how people react when I put them on the spot."

"Did she lie about anything?"

Steve thought for several seconds before he answered. "She's a tough one to read. What do you think? Did you pick up on any deception?"

Kate took her time before answering. "Nothing big, but I did notice she answered more than one of your questions with a question of her own."

Steve nodded. "For some people that's a habit—for others it's intentional because they don't want to answer. Four minutes wasn't enough time to make a determination one way or the other."

"Will you need to interview her again?"

Steve raised his shoulders and let them fall. "It depends on how the rest of the investigation goes." The air conditioner blew and the computer monitor hummed, but otherwise the exam room became quiet. "How would you like to interview Dr. Melody alone?"

"I hope you're joking."

"I'm serious. You went through a nightmare of a marriage and she's a bitter divorcée. If you're willing, get Melody to talk about her marriage to Chris and, more importantly, why she's so angry. Remember, we're working on two separate cases, with Chris and Melody as the common threads."

"This isn't a novel. I wouldn't know what to say."

"Then pretend it is a novel. Here, take this." He handed her a miniature recorder. "Do you have a pocket on your blouse?"

"Only in my slacks."

"That will do. Do you see the record button?"

"Yes."

"Put the recorder in your pocket and press that button when Dr. Melody turns the door knob to enter. Try to remain still."

"Is this legal?"

"Texas is a single party consent state. Heather and I record conversations all the time and we haven't been arrested yet."

Kate blew out a full breath. "Is there anything else you want me to ask about?"

"Start by noticing she's not wearing a wedding band. Show her your ring finger. You're a brilliant storyteller. Tell your story and sit back and let her tell you hers. Use open-ended questions and leading statements if you have to. Pretend you're writing dialog."

"What if she clams up?"

"She won't. There's enough anger inside Melody to fill two chapters in your next book." Steve moved toward the door. "I hear Melody's footsteps coming this way, so I'll go to the waiting room. Good luck."

Steve closed the door behind him. "Dr. Melody? That must be you. I recognize the scent of your soap. There's a very special friend of mine waiting for you to examine her eyes. Her name is Kate Bridges."

"The receptionist already gave me a heads-up that a famous author is here. I see on her chart she's from Miami. How do you know her?"

"Heather and I met her at a writer's conference that turned into a murder investigation. She's trying to teach me how to write, but she doesn't have a very good pupil."

Melody lowered her voice. "Any progress on the investigations?"

"Heather's mother passed away, so she's in Boston for the funeral. That's put me a little behind, but we're gaining ground a little at a time."

"That's good to hear. I'd better go in and introduce myself to the celebrity."

Steve tapped his way toward the waiting room, thinking about how Melody had used the plural 'investigations' when she asked about progress. Perhaps she still cared for Chris enough to think about his business suffering. Or, could it be she wanted to check on possible delays in child support payments? If Kate interviewed as well as she wrote, he'd know later today.

Steve waited a long time before Kate collected him in the waiting room. They didn't speak until Kate came to a halt on the sidewalk. "Hold up a minute, I need to put on my sunglasses."

"Do we need to call Uber?" he asked.

"Why would we?"

"Didn't you have your eyes dilated?"

"I'm wearing my sunglasses over a pair of those dark roll-up things they give patients. I picked up two if I need another. I should be able to drive with no trouble."

"Why does the phrase *the blind leading the blind* come to mind?"

Kate's laugh bounced off the glass and metal of the exterior of the building, followed by, "This is all part of the adventure. Besides, I need to get you back for leaving me hanging... twice."

19

Steve suggested Kate take them home after leaving Melody's practice. She readily agreed, but asked, "Do you want me to tell you what she said?"

He shook his head. "I'd rather you concentrate on driving. I'll listen to the tape once we get there safely." Steve then turned to face her as she drove. "Thank you for recording your conversation with Melody. I probably shouldn't have asked you to do it. In case you haven't noticed, I get wrapped up in these investigations and get a form of mental tunnel vision."

"Writers call that being in the flow. Sometimes I don't hear my phone ringing if I'm on a critical scene in the story."

"I haven't learned to do that with my writing; but it describes how I get once the pieces of a crime puzzle come together. Don't be surprised if I need to be alone and think. In fact, expect to be on your own when we get back to the condos. I'll take the recording back to my bedroom and listen to it several times."

Kate placed her hand on his arm. "Don't worry about me. I brought my office with me and all this sleuthing has me behind on word count, editing, and correspondence. To tell you the truth, I hope we don't have anywhere to go for the rest of the day."

"Nothing but brain work is on the calendar for the rest of today and tomorrow. There's a lot to digest and Heather should be at a point where she needs something to do or she'll pick a fight with Jack or her father."

Kate gave one of her soft chuckles. "It must be the Irish blood in her." She pulled her hand away. "Now that you've given me the brush off, are we going our separate ways the rest of the day?"

"Come over for lunch. We can mine the refrigerator for treasures untold. Otherwise, we'll do our own thing."

"Am I cooking lunch?"

"I can't guarantee what kind of cheese or lunchmeat you'll get on your sandwich."

"I'll make the sandwiches," said Kate. "You're responsible for supper. I like sushi."

Once home, Steve told Max to help Kate write her story while he shuffled back to his bedroom, stretched out on the bed, and turned on the tape recorder. He listened to the recording he made of the four minutes allotted to him by Dora Chen. It didn't take long before he had every word memorized. He recorded the audio from the tiny tape recorder into his computer so he could send the conversation to Heather.

He turned on the recorder to listen to Kate's discussion with Dr. Melody. Their twenty-two-minute talk aired a lot of dirty laundry for both women. He thought about trying to give Heather the Cliff's Notes of the conversation, but it was too much for him to memorize word for word. Heather would get the full recording of both women baring their souls and sorrows.

With both recordings and a brief message sent to Heather, he stretched out on the bed. After listening to the two women's grievances against ex-husbands, thoughts of Maggie and their years of happiness came calling. They were a welcome relief. He gave thanks for all they'd shared, interlaced his fingers over his chest, and went to sleep.

Steve awakened to the sound of his cell phone announcing a phone call from Heather. He'd placed it within reach on the comforter, convinced she'd want to discuss the two interviews once she listened to them. He cleared his throat. "Hello, Heather."

"You sound like a bullfrog. Caught you sleeping, didn't I?"

"Guilty. Did you listen to the recordings?"

"I did. Good catch on Dora Chen being an optometrist back in South Korea. Was that a lucky guess?"

Steve crossed his fingers. "That bit of genius came about from years of study, and ten thousand hours of interviewing the most devious characters in the annals of crime."

"I was right. You took a chance and lady luck showed up."

Steve uncrossed his fingers. "How much free time do you have?"

Heather gave a snort. "Time? I'm swimming in it."

"Good. There're some things I'd like you to do. First, dive deeper into Dora Chen's background. Verify she was an optometrist in South Korea, why she left, and why she isn't an optometrist here."

"I have contacts in South Korea I can call. What else?"

"Something occurred to me today when I asked Dora if another optometrist or a corporation was looking to purchase Melody's practice and retail shop."

"I've been thinking about the possibilities of that type of investment since Chris mentioned he might be interested in selling at some point," said Heather. "In fact, I put both practices and stores on my list of potential businesses to buy."

Steve gave a quick, "Right. If you're interested, how many other entrepreneurs are thinking the same thing?"

Heather waited an extra second to respond. "If you couldn't hear that, I hit my forehead with the palm of my hand. How can my brain be so dense? This could be the motive for the burglary that had me stumped. Individuals and corporations pull all sorts of stunts to discover the profitability of a company before they buy them."

Steve scooted higher on his pillow. "It could also explain the mystery of the hot pepper juice in Mattie Arnold's eye, and how quickly the television crew responded. It's likely someone wanted to drive down the price of Chris's business."

Heather took her turn. "That could be why the only thing taken from Melody's eyeglass store was tax records. Whoever's trying to buy the businesses needs to know the true worth so they don't bid too high or too low."

Steve appreciated how quick Heather's mind worked once she caught a scent, but he needed to rein her in. "Those are only theories at this point. If you can, snoop around the corporate world and see if any companies are looking to expand. Also, ask Jack to speak to Chris and see if anyone has approached him to sell. Chris might also know if anyone approached Melody recently."

A triplet of taps on the door interrupted the conversation. Steve told his phone to go to speaker. "Come in, Kate."

"Lunch is ready. I looked in on you earlier, but..."

"It's all right. Come in and say hi to Heather."

"Hello, Heather. I'm so sorry to hear about your mother. I know you being there is a big help to your father."

"Thank you, Kate. I understand Steve is trying to turn you into a gumshoe."

"I'll leave that to you professionals. I'm not sure I have what it takes."

"I listened to your interview with Dr. Melody. You did a spectacular job."

"All I did was prime the pump. She needed to talk. I guess it's true what they say about not really knowing someone until you live with them."

Steve interrupted before the two women went into details. "Heather, lunch is ready, so you know what that means."

"I certainly do. You're finished talking."

"Any questions?"

"No. You gave me my homework assignments."

Kate spoke up. "I forgot to ask when the funeral will be."

"The day after tomorrow, at 2:00 p.m. Jack and I will fly back that night."

Steve asked, "What will you do tomorrow?"

"Nothing outside the home. Father didn't like it that Jack and I went out last night. Oh well, I have plenty to keep me busy today and we'll be home soon."

After the usual salutations, Steve waited until the phone made its distinct sound of a call ending. He swung his feet off the bed and whispered, "The calm before the storm."

"What's that?" asked Kate.

"Nothing important."

KATE TOOK A PHONE CALL BEFORE SERVING LUNCH. SHE walked outside, and came back a few minutes later, closing the door harder than necessary. "Did you want iced tea or coffee with your lunch?" asked Kate with quick, chopped words.

Steve didn't need to think. "Iced tea with the meal and coffee later." He then stayed silent as she prepared their meal.

They settled on opposite sides of the table. Kate gave instructions. "I cut your sandwich in half and it's on your plate from twelve o'clock to three o'clock. There's coleslaw at six o'clock. Potato chips are at nine."

"Perfect," said Steve. He thought about the word and changed his response. "Almost perfect."

A note of impatience entered Kate's voice. "Did I put things in the wrong place or forget something you wanted?"

Steve raised a palm. "Sorry, I wasn't talking about the meal. Sometimes my mouth has trouble catching up with my mind."

"What were you thinking about?"

"The case, and how I misjudged Chris Craddock." He heard a potato chip crunch from across the table. "I listened to your conversation with Melody. Give me your thoughts on the bitterness she expressed."

Steve picked up his sandwich and took a bite while Kate either gathered her thoughts or finished chewing and swallowing. He couldn't tell, but he'd learned not to rush people, especially during a meal.

"To begin," said Kate, "it surprised me it wasn't the tryst with Sandi Fields that led to the demise of their marriage. It didn't help, but he did enough to doom their marriage long before that took place. In fact, she'd already filed for divorce and had a court date by then."

"This is a great sandwich," said Steve. "I love dill pickle slices on them, but it's hard for me to tell what kind is in the jar without tasting them first. I need to figure out a way to tell the jars apart."

"I thought we were talking about Melody and Chris."

"Sorry. I'll stuff my face while you talk about Chris."

"If I do all the talking, you'll finish your meal in no time. Then, you'll want to think instead of talk, and this meal will be Kate giving a monologue while you get lost in your thoughts." She enunciated her words with more clarity. "I eat alone every day, so pleasant conversation is a treat for me. You want my thoughts on Melody and Chris? Fine. I want to hear your thoughts, too. It's called dialogue."

Steve leaned back. "Have you been writing a scene with a lot of tension and conflict?"

"I wish." Kate took in a full breath and let it out in a rush. "My publisher wants me to change the storyline of the book I'm writing. It's the third in a series with the first two published. They think this one isn't spicy enough for the modern audience. If I make the changes they want, the book will seep into a different genre and my readers will be furious. It's a stupid idea."

"What will you do?"

"I told my agent to tell them to.... never mind what I told her." Kate took in another long breath. "This is why I have an agent. She'll call the publisher and negotiate. We'll go back and forth for a week or two and we'll either come to a compromise or I'll refuse to finish the book and have to return my advance." She paused. "It rarely comes to that. More than likely, the publication committee had a bad day because someone's book flopped or another publisher hit the jackpot with something smutty and they're chasing the market."

"Take a bite," said Steve. "It's my turn."

That earned a chuckle. "Well done. Unlike most men your age, you're teachable."

"Let's get back to the case," said Steve. "When I listened to the recording, I was surprised to hear Melody tell you Chris's gambling was one of the main reasons for their divorce. I should have known he had a problem when he made a silly bet to see who could save the most money on a cruise."

Steve took a bite of slaw and Kate took over. "Think of all the things he did to win that bet."

Steve nodded. "He chose an inside cabin, didn't go on any excursions, and did all kinds of activities on the ship to earn bonus prizes."

"Most men I know wouldn't be too keen on the games and contests they have on cruises. I wonder how he stayed out of the casino."

Steve had a potato chip up to his mouth but didn't pop it in. Instead, he lowered his hand. "Who says he didn't gamble? Didn't Melody tell us he'd say or do anything to catch a cheap flight to Vegas?"

"Not only Vegas, but anywhere with gambling."

Steve nodded. "If he'll do almost anything to go gamble, it's my guess he wouldn't be able to resist the temptation of it on the ship, nor would he see any reason to resist it. You and I need to have a talk with Chris and find out more about this mini-vacation."

"Do you need to call Heather and have her get a more complete story of Chris's onboard activities?"

Steve shook his head. "Not yet. She has enough on her plate until they return."

The two continued the meal in silence. Despite Kate's stated desire for dialogue, Steve sensed she needed periods of time to digest theories as much as he did. They pushed their plates away at the same time.

"What else impressed you about what Melody said?" asked Steve.

"I admire her for doing all she could to save their business. Her retail store covered the practice until she became an optometrist. Then in an effort to stem the flow of money going out, she took over the books for both businesses. Even so, Chris still managed to siphon money from them. Melody is in a tight spot. She's still in love with Chris, but has to protect herself and her children from financial ruin."

Steve took his turn. "In the ultimate act of protection, she divorced him; but didn't give up on him. She got the house and a huge child support settlement in exchange for fronting some of the money to set him up in practice."

Kate's sighed. "She's still protecting him by demanding monthly payments for child support along with a hefty loan repayment to her. If she's telling the truth, she's saving a portion of that to give him if he ever straightens up."

Steve finished the thought. "If she didn't, he'd gamble away his livelihood and her money."

Kate reached for Steve's plate and stacked it on top of hers. "Does this bring you any closer to solving who's responsible for Cleo Stanley's death, or who tampered with the bottle of eye drops in Chris's office?"

Steve shrugged. "Some cases you solve by discovering who did the crime. With others, it's a game of musical chairs. You eliminate all the suspects but two. Whoever doesn't get eliminated at the end loses."

"Is Chris the loser in this case?"

Steve pushed himself up from the table. "The music's still playing, and no one's out yet."

"Does that include Melody?"

"The suspects are still Melody, Chris, Sandi Fields, Dora Chen, Bryson Wayne and Cindy Green. We might need to add to the list."

"Who?"

"Some faceless corporation intent on expansion and willing to steal tax records and tamper with eye drops." Steve paused. "We need to take Chris and Detective Hall out for dinner. It's time to verify what Melody told you."

"Won't that be awkward?"

Steve took his glass to the sink. "Homicide is an awkward business."

20

Heather looked at Jack over her computer screen as he entered the library. She gave him a wink and a smile. "We have something to do other than listen to my father drone on about how a new Fed coin will replace cryptocurrencies."

Jack took a seat in the chair beside her. "He's a visionary. What was it he said? 'You have to know where the puck's going in order to stay in front of the competition?'"

"His favorite hockey metaphor. He stole it from a famous player."

"My job focuses on the past. It's much simpler."

Heather pushed her lips to one side. "What do you mean?"

Jack settled in a leather chair the color of a fat cigar and thrust his feet out. "A defense attorney represents people for crimes they've already committed, or at least for something someone did. Businesses focus on the present and the future. Because you're a private investigator, an attorney, and a business-woman, you think in all three realms: past, present, and future."

Heather turned her head. "This interests me. Keep talking."

"You and your father base your success on what's going to be hot in the future. You and Steve have to backtrack in time and discover who did what and when. To a large extent, that's what I do, too. In addition, for your business, you have to know what's going on with current market conditions and what's trending. All I'm saying is, it takes a very special person to do all three."

Heather turned toward him. "Are you coming on to me?"

He leaned in her direction. "What if I am?"

"Then I'd say you're sitting too far away."

Jack rose and sat on the couch next to her. "Is this better?"

"Much better. Now you can see my computer screen and I'll explain what we need to work on this afternoon."

A deep moan came from Jack. "I need an icepack for my bruised ego."

She cupped his face between her hands, and planted a long kiss on his lips. His eyes remained closed after she pulled away and he said, "Now I need a cold shower and an ice pack."

Heather took in a deep breath and faced her computer screen. "Eyes on the screen, counselor. There's a homicide to solve. Who knows, you might pick up a client."

"Clients I can find. Kisses from the most alluring woman I've ever met are harder to come by."

She ran her hand down his face, wanted to say she loved him, but backed away. "We have two assignments. The first is to do more background research on a suspect, Dora Chen. She's Dr. Melody's assistant. Steve tricked her into saying she'd been an optometrist in South Korea. We're to verify that and find out when and why she came to the USA. Also, why isn't she an optometrist here?"

Jack nodded. "How will you do that?"

"I'll start with people I know in the State Department, but that probably won't get all the info we need. I'll also have to call people I know in Seoul. Because of the time difference, I'll leave most of what I need to do until later this evening and start with the second thing Steve wants."

"What's that?"

"Research on the business side of optometrists' offices and stores that sell eyeglasses. Steve thinks there could be companies interested in taking over Melody and Chris's practices and retail shops. Having never worn glasses, I know little about the big players in the field."

"What do you want me to do?"

"Call Chris and find out if it's common for big companies to take over individual practices. Ask him if anyone ever approached him to sell. Concentrate on the near-term, but ask about inquiries from years ago. See if he knows if anyone's approached Melody since their divorce."

"I need my laptop."

She nodded. "It will help speed things up if we both did web searches on the companies. I'll make a list and we'll divide them."

"Between the phone calls and the research, this could take all day and night."

She lifted her eyebrows and showed a full smile. "There's thirteen hours' time difference between here and South Korea. We'll work today on the research and the stateside phone calls until dinner, rest, and be back here at midnight. The phone calls to Korea shouldn't take too long. Then we can review before we turn in."

He gave her a sideways look. "Review. That word could have more than one meaning."

She repeated the first kiss she gave him. "You'll leave smiling." She paused. "Love you."

"I'm smiling already."

THE NEXT MORNING, HEATHER AWOKE TO THUNDER AND streaks of lightening. It should have been a sunny summer day in Boston to match her upbeat mood. Rain splattered against her bedroom windows, leaving trails that would soon run off to the Atlantic Ocean. This brought thoughts of her youth and sailing. What thrills she experienced in summer squalls that popped up in the late afternoons.

After stretching in bed, Heather mentally reviewed the phone calls and Internet searches she and Jack had made the preceding day. All went according to the plan they'd sketched out, with good progress made on the investigation. Jack contacted Chris and was told regional and nationwide companies sometimes looked to take over existing practices and retail stores. Each company had their own criteria for square footage, location, and potential profitability. Chris said he had ignored inquiries, preferring to remain independent. He didn't know if anyone approached Melody after the divorce.

Putting everything together, Heather concluded the profit margin on designer eyeglasses could be well worth her while to dig deeper. If she was interested, how many other companies might look at Melody's business? Not so much with Chris's because his wasn't prospering. She'd need to look at Chris's books to see how much profit he was gambling away.

While brushing her teeth, she thought about the calls she'd made to South Korea. Her sources promised to email the results of their inquiries about Dora Chen. All the wheels were turning and it wouldn't be long before she had a full report to give to Steve. She considered calling him, but decided instead to think about the recent midnight rendezvous with Jack. Pleasant thoughts, indeed.

After showering and dressing for the day, she went downstairs for breakfast with her father. Jack came out of his room as she approached the stairway. They yawned at the same time.

"Sleep well?" he asked.

"Excellent quality, but quantity left a little to be desired." She took his hand. "And you?"

He gave her a roguish grin. "Perhaps the next time we stay up past midnight, we could forgo business altogether."

"Speaking of business, we're late for breakfast. Father is unbearable when I'm late."

Jack took a step toward the stairs. "I'll race you."

She burst into the dining room ahead of Jack. Grinning, she said, "I win." She felt like skipping, the way she did as a child when her parents weren't looking. "Good morning, Father. I hope you slept well."

Her smile faded when his scowling countenance appeared over the top of the newspaper. It was then she noticed the black armband on the sleeve of his suit coat. She tried again, in a more refined voice. "Good morning, Father. I hope you slept well."

He went back to reading his paper. "A little decorum would be in order. Did you forget tomorrow is the day we bury your mother?"

She reacted the same way she did in college. Her chin came up, her shoulders went back, and her fists tightened. "Of course, I didn't forget. How could you say such a thing?"

He took his time folding the newspaper and laying it beside his empty coffee cup. "It seemed a reasonable question to pose to a daughter who was up at all hours of the night and morning."

Jack took a step forward, but Heather held out her hand to stop him. "You might like to know that I was making phone calls to South Korea. Then Jack helped me do research on a homicide investigation Steve and I are working on."

Her father raised a single eyebrow. She'd seen him demonstrate the gesture all her life. It meant he doubted she'd told the truth. She had to admit, if only to herself, that she hadn't come close to telling the whole truth.

"I've made hundreds of phone calls to South Korea in my life, but I can't remember them taking two and a half hours."

"Once again, Father, I'm not you. Besides, in case you haven't noticed, I'm a grown woman."

"Who should be in mourning."

Jack cleared his throat. "Mr. McBlythe, you're right, and it's my fault we were in the library at such an hour. I apologize.

Perhaps my presence here isn't a good idea. It might be best if I left you and Heather to grieve in private."

Her father reached in the pocket of his coat, withdrew an airline ticket and slid it across the table. "That would be best."

"No!" shouted Heather. "I'll not permit this."

Jack grabbed her shoulders and turned her toward him. "It's all right. We'll talk when you get home."

Her father's voice sounded from the head of the table. "This is Heather's home. It always was, and always will be."

Jack released his grip on her and turned to the stone-faced patriarch. "That's up to Heather to decide. You can keep your ticket, Mr. McBlythe. I can pay my own way." He turned to Heather. "It's probably best this way. I love you, but we both need time to think." He kissed her cheek. "Good-bye, Heather."

Stunned into silence, Heather's feet seemed stuck in quicksand. She caught up with Jack at the front door just as her father's butler handed him his suitcase. Through her tears, she asked, "Harold, did Father tell you to pack his things?"

"Please don't be angry with me, Miss Heather."

Jack opened the door. In the circular driveway stood a waiting cab. More evidence of her father's meticulous planning.

"Jack," cried Heather. "Wait for me."

Jack turned and gave a weak wave. "You're needed here. Take care of your father."

As if to spite her, a sunbeam burst through the parting clouds while the rain continued to pelt down. She blinked against the water, tears, and bright sun. In a matter of seconds, Jack's taxi rounded the corner and disappeared from sight. Heather ran to her room and stayed the rest of the morning with her head buried in a pillow.

Noon came and went, with only the cook coming to bring her a light lunch, which she didn't eat. Thoughts of Jack waiting at the airport filled her mind. To mock her even further, the clouds cleared so she knew there would be no rain delays for his flight. She imagined him on a crowded airplane, headed south-west, back to the sultry heat of Texas.

By early evening, she'd shed three decades of tears. Hunger pangs caused her stomach to rumble. She went to the kitchen where Rose, the cook, welcomed her with a hot cup of tea and soft words. The woman wore her apron with pride, and had done so all Heather's life. The only thing different about Rose was her girth. She'd been a wide woman, a victim of her Irish cooking, heavy on the potatoes. The doctor told her she'd be on insulin if she didn't slim down, so she converted to salads.

"Hot tea may not be what ya' want, lass. But it's better for ya' than what comes out of a bottle of spirits. I've kept your supper warm—a nice bowl of Irish stew with plenty of vegetables and fresh rolls."

Comforted by the familiarity of the cook's warm brogue, Heather's lips turned up in a half-smile. "Thank you. Has Father already eaten?"

"If he did, it wasn't anything from this kitchen. He left after lunch. I haven't seen him since. Worried and hurt, he was."

Heather let out a quick snort. "He probably went to the office."

"Not dressed the way he was."

Heather countered with, "He had on a suit when I saw him."

She shrugged. "Must'a changed. Could be he's visitin' the docks. That's where he and your mam would go when they needed to talk out their worries. There's somethin' about the water that calms him."

"Perhaps he'll fall in."

"No need to talk like that. His heart beats loud for ya'. Almost as loud as your mam's did. God rest her soul."

Heather swallowed what seemed like a boiled egg in her throat. She whispered, "Mother." Then, she rose from the small table in the kitchen where she'd spent so many days as a child. "I seem to have lost my appetite."

"I've made things for a late-night snack. Here, take a few of these low-carb cookies with ya'. I don't tell your father what's in 'em, and he thinks they're grand."

At ten o'clock, Heather broke her fast. That's when she noticed her phone hadn't rung or beeped all day. When did she turn it off and what had she missed? She looked at it and put it back on the nightstand without powering it on. This night belonged to Mother and Jack.

21

I t took more makeup than usual to cover the dark circles under Heather's eyes. She purposefully made her arrival to breakfast late, hoping to avoid her father, doubting she'd ever forgive him for the way he treated Jack. She shouldn't have wasted her time practicing what to say. An empty seat, a clean plate, and an undisturbed newspaper next to a china coffee cup with saucer all bore witness that he'd skipped breakfast.

The sideboard held shining chafing dishes, keeping a full breakfast warm. Heather settled for whole wheat toast, a pat of butter, and a small scoop of scrambled eggs. She rejected the breakfast meats and a cup of fresh fruit. After settling herself at the table, she picked at the eggs, choked down half a slice of toast and drank only one cup of coffee. The house matched her mood: dark and silent, as if the materials the craftsman had labored over during construction knew this day would come. It was the home's way of showing respect to the matriarch.

Heather went to her room and gazed out the window into the back garden. How many times had she seen the same view, and how many times did she long to be somewhere else? A soft drizzle muted the scene. "Funeral weather," she said.

She turned and noticed her phone on the nightstand.

Heather powered it on and a blinking blue light alerted her to at least one missed message or call. "One? More likely to be thirty." She ignored the notifications and called her pilot with instructions to have her plane ready to leave that evening. "I wish I could give you a more exact time, but I'm not sure how long the service at the church and the burial will take. I may have to come back to the house, but I want to leave as soon as possible."

"That might not work," said the pilot. "There's a glitch with the backup radio. The repair technician is busy until sometime this afternoon."

Heather let out a deep sigh. "Do what you can. I'll call for an update after the graveside services."

She disconnected the call, shut the phone down again and looked around the room. An involuntary shiver caused her to hug herself as a sensation of not belonging came over her. She whispered, "This is not my home. I'm not sure it ever was."

A knock on the door brought her back to herself. "Come in."

Her father appeared, dressed in his pajamas, robe, and house shoes. She couldn't remember the last time she'd seen him wearing bedclothes. He looked away, avoiding eye contact after closing the door behind him. "I... uh..."

He looked up, and she beheld red-rimmed eyes.

"I wanted to make sure you knew the schedule for the day."

Heather stood straight, as if someone had covered her in quick drying cement. She spoke with emotionless words. "I was wondering when I needed to be ready. I'm sure you have my every move planned."

He nodded. "Would you prefer I tell you or give you the printed itinerary?"

"Printed is my preference."

Her father cleared his throat. "This is rather hard to say, but I expect you to sit at my side during the memorial service and stand by me at graveside."

"Of course," she said with clipped words. "Propriety demands it." She paused. "I'll be leaving as soon as possible, but I learned this morning my plane needs a minor repair."

"Like I said yesterday, this is your home. You may come and go as you please."

It took everything in Heather not to say that this mansion stopped being her home a long time ago, if it ever was. She also stuffed down the desire to say she had no intention of ever coming here again after he treated Jack like an uninvited salesman. But she thought of her mother and bit her tongue. Instead, she said, "I'll tell Rose not to expect me for breakfast tomorrow."

Her father responded with a nod, turned, and left.

If she thought she'd exhausted her supply of tears, Heather was sorely mistaken. Something had torn in the fabric of her life yesterday. Life would be different from now on.

THE FUNERAL PASSED IN FRONT OF HER AS A BLUR OF SIGHTS and sounds; high church with an overpowering organ and an aged priest who spoke with perfect diction. Her eyes stayed locked on her mother's casket. She was glad her personal assistant included a somber hat with a black veil. The surprise came when her father abandoned his stoicism, allowed silent tears to slide down his cheeks, and took her hand. She concluded her parents had deep feelings for each other, somewhere under the layers of society-imposed expectations.

Soggy graveside services kept the crowd down, which she counted as a small blessing in an otherwise dreadful day. The burial service lasted a mercifully short amount of time, which also suited her. She dutifully placed a single flower on her mother's coffin and allowed an unknown man with an umbrella to shield her from the mist. She walked to a waiting limousine where her father joined her, and they made a wordless journey back to the place that had once been her home.

She'd memorized the printed itinerary, which called for a reception with some of her father's most influential business associates and political luminaries. It proved to be the acid test of all her careful training in the social graces. She appeared to all as the dutiful, loving daughter of one of Boston's most influential men. After an hour and a half of making the rounds and receiving near-identical expressions of sympathy, she escaped to the sanctuary of her bedroom, where she immediately activated her phone and called her pilot. "Tell me the radio's fixed and you have the plane ready to go."

"All fixed, and I've filed our flight plan. We're waiting for you."

"I'll leave in the next ten minutes."

With her plan in place to make her escape through the back door, she called the family chauffeur. She slipped out of the black dress and put on leggings, a long, comfy knit shirt and cross-trainer shoes.

A tap on the door came when she snapped her suitcase shut.

"I came to give you a hand," said the chauffeur.

"Thanks. Let's go down the back stairs and through the kitchen."

"Just like old times," said the man, who was about the same age as her father. "You always preferred to use the back door."

"Only this time I'm not sneaking out."

"Of course not, Miss Heather."

The lid to the trunk of the black Mercedes made a distinct sound when it closed, like an auditory exclamation mark. Heather turned to the man who'd driven her to ballet classes when she was four. "I'll ride up front with you, if you don't mind."

"As you wish. You never did like the back seat."

"I like to see where I'm going."

Heather glanced at the house a final time as they passed the conservatory. The man she saw looking out the window might have been her father, but the mist-fogged windows made it impossible to tell. She turned her head and looked out the passenger side. Her words came out with a hesitation. "Did you take Father somewhere last night?"

"I did."

"Can you tell me where?"

"Do you promise to make it our secret like we used to?"

"I won't tell Father."

He wheeled around a corner. "We went to Fenway Park."

Heather jerked her head to the left. "My Father went to see the Red Sox play last night? I didn't know he ever went to baseball games."

"It's been a recent development. He and your mother started going after they returned from seeing you in Texas. Five of us went last night. The Sox beat the Yankees five to four. Then we went to the Bull and Finch Pub, where we had a late supper and a few rounds from the bar."

Heather shook her head. "He must have a big deal cooking and needed to entertain clients."

"I couldn't say. None of the three men were from Boston."

After fighting their way through traffic, Heather boarded her twin-engine jet as the copilot and chauffeur loaded suitcases and hanging clothes. The engines came to life as she buckled her seatbelt, pulled up a retractable tabletop, and placed her laptop on it.

"Care for something to drink before we take off?" asked the copilot.

"Not yet. It seems I have about fifty emails to go through." She looked up as the copilot walked away. "By the way, nice ball cap."

He turned, took it off, and smiled. "Sorry. I forgot I had it on. I'm not that much of a Red Sox fan, but I can't stand the Yankees."

Heather returned the smile as she looked down at her computer screen.

The plane screamed down the runway and went airborne as

Heather shuffled through the emails, filing or deleting as she went. One caught her eye, and she reached for the corded phone beside her. She punched in the overseas number and waited. It rang five times before she realized the time difference between 7:00 p.m. Boston time and whatever that was in South Korea.

"Hello, Ms. McBlythe."

"I hope I didn't wake you, Mr. Cho."

"No, no. I'm so sorry to hear about your mother. Please accept my condolences."

"That's very kind." She paused, remembering her mother's face. "I wanted to thank you for getting back to me concerning Dora Chen."

"Yes. She was an optometrist in good standing. She practiced for several years before marrying a United States serviceman. She applied for and received a work visa."

"No criminal history?"

"None."

"Did anything stand out to you as odd or unusual?"

"Only one thing. She left this country with a large amount of money."

Heather reread portions of the email as she searched for another question to ask. "One last thing. Can you think of any reason Dora Chen isn't an optometrist here in the States?"

"No. It surprises me she isn't."

"Thank you. Please say hello to your wife and children. I hope they remember me."

"All I had to say was the woman with auburn hair called and the little one squealed. I hope you didn't mind them wanting to touch your hair. It's a cultural thing here to touch hair that's as beautiful as yours."

"I took it as a compliment. Thank you so much for looking into this matter for me."

"Dr. Chen isn't in any kind of trouble, is she?"

"The police are eliminating suspects. This information may help a great deal."

Again, he chuckled. "Your father used to tell me he was afraid you'd turn into a grown-up version of Nancy Drew. I didn't know what he meant until I read the books."

"My father is realizing his worst fears."

"He's an honorable man who loves you very much. I hurt for him on the loss of his wife and your mother."

Heather tried to speak but could only squeak out a quick, "Thank you. You're very kind."

After hanging up, she placed her laptop in the seat Jack should have been sitting in and made her way to the small galley at the front of the plane. She opened the door to the refrigerator, withdrew a Coke Zero, and returned to her seat.

Her next phone call went to Steve, who answered on the second ring. As was sometimes his habit, he spoke what was on his mind without a word of greeting. "It sounds like you're homeward bound. How are you faring?"

"Not good."

"Did you get any sleep last night?"

"No."

"Are you drinking coffee?"

"A Coke with no sugar or caffeine."

"Yuk."

His reaction made her smile. Then he said, "Put your computer away, pull down the shades, turn off the lights, cover up with a blanket, and go to sleep. It might help if you pretended you were on that catamaran we talked about."

"I have information to give you about Dora Chen and businesses that might be interested in taking over Melody and Chris's practices and stores."

"Those can wait until tomorrow. Kate and I are meeting Chris and Detective Hall for dinner. We're driving to the restaurant now. I'm hoping to get a better read of Chris."

Heather heard tires squeal. Kate let out a string of words, the nicest being "idiot."

"What happened?" asked Heather.

Kate's voice sounded loud and clear. "Some guy in an old pickup truck cut me off so he could pull into a fried chicken restaurant. Sorry about the colorful language."

Steve chuckled. "That must be good chicken. I'll have to try it." He paused. "Speaking of food, I'll expect you and Kate for breakfast at my place bright and early tomorrow morning."

"Are you sure you don't want my update tonight?"

"I can tell by your voice you've been through enough for one day. We'll start fresh in the morning. The weather forecast is for thunderstorms tonight and sunny, hot days from here on."

"That will be a welcome relief."

22

———

Kate brought the rental to a stop with no further traffic mishaps. The restaurant Steve chose specialized in comfort food that came in large portions. Once again, he fully intended to take enough home for tomorrow's lunch. She placed her hand on his arm before he could unbuckle his seat belt. "I apologize for my language."

He waved off the *mea culpa*. "I slammed Maggie's hand in a car door once. Her sailor's vocabulary was more extensive than I thought."

"I appreciate you minimizing my failing. I hope you don't think I make a habit of using salty words like that."

Steve rubbed his chin. "Something happens to most people when they get behind the wheel of a car. My life is much more peaceful now that I can't see all the poor decisions drivers make." He paused. "That's not to say I wouldn't like to have my sight back, but I've learned to appreciate not having to battle traffic."

"Do you think it will be less stressful when they perfect self-driving cars?"

"It remains to be seen how many people want it," said Steve as he depressed the latch on his seatbelt. "Some will disable it so they can beat the other guy to the next stoplight. There's a spark of rebellion in everyone."

"What do you rebel against?"

"Hunger... and sitting in a vehicle with the engine off in the middle of the summer." This earned him another of Kate's laughs. He'd miss those when she went back to Florida.

Inside, Steve lifted his chin when he heard Detective Hall say, "Follow me. I came early to make sure we didn't have to wait on a table."

"Is Dr. Chris here yet?" asked Steve.

"Not yet, but there's ten minutes still before the time you told him to arrive."

"What about Jack Blackstock?"

"Let's get seated before we talk."

Kate led him through the restaurant. The rattle of dishes, the din of multiple conversations, and the occasional outburst of laughter created something of a musical score.

After weaving through tables, Kate slowed to a stop. "It's a round table with five chairs. How do you want to arrange us?"

Steve had already worked it out. "You sit on my right. Detective Hall, you'll be on my left. That will give both of you a clear view of Chris. Put Jack next to him."

Chairs slid on a floor that seemed to be made of slick concrete. Detective Hall spoke in a loud whisper. "Why did you include Chris's attorney?"

Steve matched his volume to that of Hall's. "Heather's my partner. I rely on her to give me accurate descriptions of people's reactions to questions. Since she's not here, I have to improvise. Jack is a logical choice since he's Heather's partner, but in a different way. He's pretty used to how I operate. Kate is a master storyteller who focuses on details. I'll be counting on both Kate and Jack to tell me the non-verbal portion of tonight's meeting. I'll listen to and record the words, but that won't paint the entire picture."

"Still," said Hall. "Jack may caution Dr. Chris not to say anything about the case."

Steve smiled. "This is the challenging part of being a private detective. Chris is our client, but we made it clear to him we're after the truth."

"I thought your job was to protect your client."

"Chris wanted us to protect his ex-wife and kids from any financial hardships. He said nothing about us protecting him."

The server came and took drink orders, putting a temporary end to the conversation. When he left, Steve asked, "What can you tell me about Cleo Stanley?"

Detective Hall continued to speak in a loud whisper. "She was married to a man who didn't deserve her."

Kate's arm brushed Steve's as she placed her napkin on her lap. "I can relate to that."

Hall continued, "Everyone I talked to said she was a good, church-going woman. Around her neighborhood, that means every time the church doors opened, she was inside. Nobody had a bad thing to say about her."

"What about her husband?" asked Steve.

"They say opposites attract. That appears to be true with Cleopatra Stanley and her husband, Pooky. Of course, that's not his real name, but nobody would know who you were talking about if you called him William."

"Arrests?" asked Steve.

"An even dozen for Pooky, and one three-year visit at the Ferguson Prison Farm when he was eighteen. Nothing serious since then, but he was no stranger to jail. Multiple public intoxication charges, misdemeanor possession arrests, shoplifting, and hot checks. I'm amazed he's been clean and sober for the last year and a half."

"Did you speak with him?"

"I went to the funeral and the dinner at church after the burial. Some of the best food I ever tasted. It was quite a celebration in a sad sort of way. The preacher, Reverend Bishop, made it clear from the pulpit it was Cleo's prayers that brought Pooky to the Lord. He and their six children stood up and shouted, 'Amen!' That got everyone going. I never heard so many *Amens* in my life as when the Reverend told the congregation to never give up on God. Singing and dancing in the aisles broke out. I tell you it was a hand-clapping going away party for Miss Cleo."

Steve couldn't help but smile. He then thought about Heather and her mother's funeral. How different it must have been from Cleo's send off.

Drinks arrived, and so did Jack and Chris. Both men asked the server to bring them iced tea. Steve spoke first, after he heard chairs move away from the table and then come back in. "Jack, have you heard from Heather?"

"Not yet."

Steve gave his head a quick nod. "You will. She called me from her airplane, wanting to give me an update on her inquiries concerning Dora Chen and the other assignment I gave her."

"Do you think we pushed her too hard?"

Steve took a drink from his glass of iced tea. "Gross. I asked for sweet tea and he brought unsweetened." He set the glass on the table. "Don't worry. Heather's asleep somewhere over Pennsylvania, dreaming of sailing the Caribbean."

"With or without me?"

"That's up to you to find out."

Kate spoke up. "I'm learning Steve has a mischievous streak in him. Don't expect too many straight answers out of him."

"Enough about me," said Steve. "You two smell like suntan lotion. Did you go golfing this afternoon?"

Jack spoke first. "I took the first flight out this morning, so I called Chris and we played nine holes."

"I couldn't get away early enough to play more," said Chris. "It's a good thing we didn't play a full eighteen. He fleeced me on all but two holes, and those we tied."

"You usually come out on top, so it was my turn. Besides, I'm not the one who insisted we bet twenty bucks per hole."

"My luck's been in the sewer ever since I put that one little drop in Mattie Arnold's eye."

"Speaking of," said Steve. "Have you heard anything from the company that manufacturers the drops?"

"Not a word. What about you, Detective Hall?"

"I'm not supposed to comment on ongoing investigations, but I'll say nothing's changed since their official denial of wrongdoing."

It was Jack's turn. "My mother said their attorneys didn't return my calls and they haven't responded to the letter I sent."

"Does that surprise you?" asked Kate.

"Not at all. It's a tactic called 'delay and hope it goes away.' They won't respond to anything less than a court filing."

Steve placed his palms on the table beside his silverware. "I wanted to ask you and Chris about that. Has Mattie Arnold's mother pursued a civil action against Chris?"

"They served me with papers this morning," said Chris.

Jack shifted in his chair. "Did it slip your mind to tell me?"

Chris immediately came back with, "Is it too much for a guy to take a break for an afternoon? In case you don't remember, things are a little stressful in my world right now."

Jack let out a huff. "I'll stop by your apartment tonight and pick them up."

"No," said Chris with too much force. "What I mean is, they're still at the office. We'll go there after supper."

The server arrived with drinks for Chris and Jack. Steve addressed the young man. "I ordered sweet tea, not unsweetened. Would you take this and bring me what I ordered?"

"There's sweetener on the table."

"I didn't realize that. Is it real sugar?"

"Uh... no."

"Is there sugar in the kitchen?"

"Yeah. I think so."

"Are there cooks in the kitchen?"

"Sure."

"Do they have spoons?"

He issued a dopey laugh. "Of course, they have spoons."

"That's wonderful. Tell them you have a grumpy, blind customer that won't leave you a tip if they don't make him half a pitcher of tea sweetened with real sugar. I'll leave it up to you to bring me a glass filled with ice and the pitcher of sweet tea."

Kate spoke next. "Your tip from all of us depends on you completing this task. He likes his tea very sweet."

While they waited, Steve used the time to inform everyone that he and Kate would meet with Heather the first thing in the morning. "She did research on the possibility of a company or corporation wanting to take over Melody's businesses."

Detective Hall shifted in his chair. "I hadn't considered that angle. Do you mind if I come over and listen?"

"Be there at seven thirty and you'll get breakfast."

Chris spoke next. "I had a couple of inquiries from optometry chain stores before I opened my practice. Also, an ophthalmologist expressed interest in buying me out, but that was during the divorce and Melody's attorney fixed it where I couldn't sell."

"Wait a minute," said Jack. "You told me yesterday you ignored the inquiries."

"Well, I... uh," said Chris. "I meant to say I was interested, but that all changed when Melody's attorney slammed on the brakes."

"Would you have sold if you could?" asked Steve.

"If the price was right, I would have. We never got that far in the negotiations."

Steve followed this thread to see where it might lead. "Is it common for ophthalmologists' to buy existing practices?"

"It isn't for this guy. He specializes in Lasik surgery."

Steve leaned back. "This is interesting."

Detective Hall spoke up. "I've seen commercials on television. Is it the doctor who has clinics all over Houston and the surrounding area?"

"Uh huh."

Steve leaned forward again. "What's his name?"

"Dr. Raymond Lee," said Chris.

"Yeah, that's him," said Detective Hall.

Steve jumped back in. "What happens to the optometrists who sell their practices?"

"The guy's an ophthalmologist, so he tries to keep on most of the staff, including the optometrists. The only caveat is, the optometrists are supposed to mention the benefits of Lasik surgery to their patients that qualify."

"I get it," said Kate. "It's like a car dealership that sends you to their back room for financing and then to another person if you need insurance."

Chris's voice sounded upbeat, even excited. "It's one-stop shopping for your vision."

Jack asked, "What's the downside?"

"The only one I could see is, the optometrist loses control over their business. For some, that's not a bad thing. Running a practice is a real pain in the neck. Add a retail store to it and it's twice the headaches. Some people have a knack for that sort of thing and others are better off working for a salary."

Steve jumped back in. "Is that what appealed to you? You don't enjoy having to deal with personnel issues, taxes, and paying the bills?"

"Melody took care of all that in my old practice. I didn't realize how good I had it until I set up my new practice and retail store."

The server arrived. "Here's your sweet tea, sir. I've already poured you a glass."

Steve eased his hand across the table until his fingertips met cold glass. He lifted it and took a drink. "That's how southern iced tea is supposed to taste. Are you ready to take our orders?"

"I have my pen in hand."

"Good. What's the special of the day?"

"Grandma's pot roast. It's a one dish meal with thick gravy, potatoes, carrots, and green beans."

"That sounds wonderful."

The server didn't move on. "Would you like me to have the cook cut everything into bite-size pieces for you?"

Steve nodded. "Your tip just went up."

Chris was last to order, then excused himself to wash his hands.

Once his footsteps faded, Steve faced Jack. "Did everything go as planned in Boston?"

"I don't think she suspects anything."

"Don't count on it. She can smell out a surprise better than anyone I know."

Kate put her hand on Steve's forearm. "With all the intrigue swirling around the table, I'd like to know what my role is supposed to be tomorrow."

Steve patted her hand. "You're to come over for breakfast with Heather, then you'll be on your own until lunch. Heather and I will meet with Melody. We need to find out who in her office has a key to the retail shop next door. After that, Heather and I will review the case and quiz each other on what we've learned."

Jack spoke next. "Please keep Mom in your prayers. She's going for a stress test Thursday."

Steve nodded. "Heather should be available to go with you. With a little luck, we'll have this case buttoned up by then."

Detective Hall shifted in his chair. "I'll say Amen to that."

23

Heather struggled to free herself from the tangled sheets. She recalled the flight home and the turbulence they hit over Louisiana and into East Texas. The dream-laden sleep Steve suggested ended with a jolt that further frayed overstretched emotions. The pilot issued belated instructions to stay buckled up and said they'd need to swing to the west to avoid a line of thunderstorms.

Once on the ground, a flat tire on her SUV awaited her. The copilot discovered the head of a screw between the treads of the Michelin tire. Her pilot and copilot were two of the best when it came to flying a corporate jet, but left something to be desired changing a tire. She finally called AAA for roadside assistance, which meant another wasted hour.

A dark condo awaited her sometime on the far side of midnight. She walked past Kate's closed door with no light seeping from the bottom, and tiptoed to her room. Trying to be quiet, she kicked off her shoes and promptly stubbed her little toe while going into the bathroom.

As the throbbing subsided, she brushed her teeth and dressed for bed without further maiming herself. A mental recording of her father dismissing Jack from his house played in amazing clarity as soon as her head hit the pillow. She tried to write his actions off to grief, but wasn't sure his heart had compassion enough to experience such a deep emotion. To make things worse, Jack hadn't called or even sent a text. Of course, she hadn't tried to get in touch with him either. She could have called him from the airplane instead of working on the case. "Priorities," she whispered. "I have to get my priorities straight or I'm going to lose him." Two hours later she fell into a fitful sleep.

A glance at the clock upon opening her eyes revealed she had seven minutes to be next door. She slipped into a summer robe, ran a brush through her tangles, and tried to remove the taste of regret with toothpaste and mouthwash. She gave herself a good look in the mirror. "I didn't think it was possible to look as rotten as I feel, but there's proof staring back at me."

She took in a deep breath, puffed out her cheeks, and let it out. "Mother would say, 'Young lady, lift that chin and pull those shoulders back.'" She followed her mother's now silent instructions.

Heather wondered if Kate had already gone next door. The answer to the unasked question came when she passed the guest bedroom and glanced in. Her houseguest had already made the bed. She also noticed Max curled in a black ball, laying on a spiral notebook in the center of the comforter. Max looked at her, issued a curled-tongue yawn, and put his head back down.

"Traitor," said Heather as she made for the front door.

She tapped on Steve's door and heard him holler for her to come in. Once she took a few steps, she could see into the kitchen and the adjoining dining room. Kate wore *her* apron emblazoned with the words, *Heather's Diner.* Steve had given it to her as a gag gift, saying she needed it more at his condo because he ate real food instead of a steady diet of salad.

Steve's exuberant voice didn't match her mood. "Good morning, sunshine. How was the flight? I listened to the weather last night. It sounded rough over East Texas."

"We had to go west and come back behind the line of storms." Heather turned. "Hello, Kate. Has Steve been behaving himself?"

Kate put a clear glass bowl on the counter. "He's an absolute terror." She wiped her hands on the apron, walked to her, drew her in with a hug, and whispered. "I'm so sorry."

"Thank you," she said, and meant it. Heather had to admit it. Kate gave hugs that left you feeling cared for.

Steve continued in a more jovial tone. "We'll need to eat and run this morning. Kate's tired of being my chauffeur, and you and I have an appointment to meet Melody at her clinic. Have you given any consideration as to how the person or persons responsible for Cleo Stanley's death got in with no sign of forced entry?"

Heather tented her hands on her hips. "I've considered nothing, absolutely nothing, about the case this morning, nor do I intend to until I have at least two cups of coffee in me."

Kate laughed. "I can fix that." She poured Heather's first mug of eye-opener and handed it to her.

Heather inhaled deeply and said, "Mmm. Perfect. What about you, Kate? Are you coming with us?"

She shook her head. "I've written the Countess of Ashcroft into a hopeless situation, and I'm not sure how she'll get out of it. If I don't rescue her this morning, she'll die of boredom."

It was Heather's turn to laugh, and it felt good. She took in the scene of Kate cooking and Steve sitting at the table in his sightless world. Kate saw life through the eyes of her characters. Steve used memories, his remaining senses, and his problem-solving mind. They looked very natural together. She sighed. Perhaps someday.

The sound of scrambled eggs hitting a hot skillet pulled Heather away from her early morning daydream. "Give me fifteen minutes after breakfast and I'll be ready to solve a murder."

"That's good," said Steve. "We have a deadline. Jack's mother is going for a stress test Thursday. We need to have this wrapped up before then."

Heather clutched her hand over her heart. "Make it twenty minutes before I'll be ready. I need to call Jack."

Was that a grin on Kate's face as she spun to stir the eggs?

***

HEATHER LED STEVE THROUGH THE WAITING ROOM OF Melody's practice. She whispered, "The room is already half-full. Are you sure Melody has time to see us?"

"She opens the waiting room thirty minutes early so new patients can get registered. Then, they go to the back where Dora Chen and one other assistant do the refractions and dilate patients' eyes. It will be twenty or thirty minutes before Melody sees anyone."

"This is quite the assembly line."

"Yep. You saw her tax returns. This is the reason she's not hurting."

A sliding glass door separating the receptionist from those waiting slid open. A woman wearing half-lensed glasses looked up over the rims. "Hello, Mr. Smiley and Ms. McBlythe. Dr. Melody's expecting you. I believe you know where her office is."

Heather nodded, and they set off for the second door on the left. It stood open, so Heather simply said, "Knock, knock."

Melody spun in her chair. "Come in, and please close the door."

Steve spoke while Heather directed him to a chair. "That's quite a crowd waiting for you. Business seems good."

"I have no complaints. We did lose two days of revenue from the business next door, but I'm running a sale and we'll catch up in no time." She took a breath. "I know this isn't a social visit, so what can I do for you?"

Steve folded his collapsible cane. "I'm curious about keys to your retail store. Who has a copy?"

Melody crossed her long legs. "I was wondering when someone would ask me about that. I only allow the opening and closing managers to have a key. Of course, I keep one on my ring and there's a spare in the key safe." She pointed to a gray metal box behind the closed door. "The receptionist and I are the only ones with keys to the safe." She paused. "That doesn't mean there aren't other keys floating around to this office and the store next door."

"Why is that?" asked Heather.

"If you've spent any time with my ex-husband, you've noticed he can be flighty. His intentions have always been good, and he's a skilled optometrist, but that's the full extent of his attention to detail. By the time our divorce became inevitable, our communication had all but ceased. I tried asking him which employees had keys to the practice, the locked cabinets, and the store. I grew tired of his evasive answers and went to all my employees and retrieved keys from the ones who didn't need them."

Steve asked, "What about Sandi Fields? Did you get the key from her?"

"She said she gave it to Chris, but I can't be sure."

Steve moved on. "I had dinner with Chris and Detective Hall last night. Chris mentioned he'd considered selling the businesses. Did you know about that?"

"That was what tipped the scales in favor of me filing. He tried to hide from me that he'd entered into negotiations for the sale. That deception was the proverbial last straw."

Heather interrupted. "How did he deceive you?"

"Chris always had his eye out for whatever would make him rich quick. He's the type of person who wants instant gratification and loathes a slow, steady rise to the top. That slick corporate guy came in wearing a Rolex, an Armani suit, and a pair of thousand-dollar shoes. He took Chris golfing. Five grand of winnings was all it took to turn Chris's head. If I hadn't filed when I did, all this would belong to someone else."

Melody's eyes pooled with tears. Not enough to run down her cheeks, but plenty to show she still had powerful feelings.

Steve allowed a few quiet seconds to pass before he pressed on. "Chris told us the guy that made the offer was an ophthalmologist in Houston looking to add LASIK surgery to the practice."

Melody nodded. "It wasn't Dr. Lee, the father, but one of his sons who wined and dined Chris. The deal wasn't as good as Chris thought. There was a large up-front down-payment, but nothing guaranteed after that. In fact, they had the right to terminate all employees, or adjust salaries, after one year."

"One more question about this Dr. Lee. Did he, anyone from his family, or a business associate, approach you to sell after your divorce?"

Melody gave her head a firm nod. "The same son that tried to make the deal with Chris. I showed him my profit-and-loss statement, which made his low-ball offer look foolish. Out of spite, I came up with a counteroffer that was three times the number of his offer, multiplied it by ten and told him that's what it would take to buy me out. I haven't heard from them since, nor do I expect to."

Heather smiled. "You're my kind of businesswoman."

"That's high praise coming from you."

Steve stood, but Melody asked him to sit down. "There's one more thing I'd like to say to you, even though it probably won't help you solve this case."

Steve sat, nodded, and said, "You never know. Let's hear it."

"I fought hard to get all the money out of Chris's hands that I could. I did it to protect him from himself. All loan repayment and part of the child support he pays goes into investments. If he ever gets the gambling monkey off his back, I'll let him have that money a little at a time. I'm also selling our home and getting something more manageable for the kids and me. Half the profit from that sale will also be his if he ever straightens out."

Steve said, "You may wait a long time before he comes around."

"I play the long game."

Heather changed the subject and hit Melody with an unrelated question, a tactic she and Steve both liked to use to check people's reactions. "Did you know Dora Chen was a licensed doctor of optometry in South Korea?"

Melody's eyes widened, then narrowed. "I should have known. Even though she defers to me, her depth of knowledge is too much for an assistant." She tilted her head. "Why hasn't she pursued her license to practice here?"

Steve said, "We were hoping you might have that answer."

Melody shook her head. "I wish Dora would. I designed this practice for two optometrists."

Heather stood and held out her hand. "Thank you for your time and your honesty."

Once outside in the blazing sun, Heather asked, "What's next?"

"Let's run by Chris's retail store and talk to Sandi Fields one more time. It bothers me there might be keys we can't account for."

24

Heather dug in her purse for her sunglasses and put them on before she started her SUV. Steve voiced his opinion about priorities. "I don't like to complain, but would you mind starting the engine and blowing some cool air before you fuss with your sunglasses, seat belt, and adjust the rearview mirror?"

"It's a habit I developed when our chauffeur taught me how to drive. You're lucky I got out of the habit of doing a walk-around of the car to check for flat tires or any other damage."

Steve gave a little grunt. "Did you know scientists have recorded temperatures of over a hundred and seventy degrees in cars?"

"It's not that hot in here."

He buckled his seat belt. "Let's not take any chances."

Heather cranked the motor and turned the air conditioner to its lowest setting and the fan on high. Steve said, "Aah" when cool air ruffled his hair.

She looked at him. "I thought you'd be in a better mood after that interview with Melody. I had her pegged as a bitter, spurned woman. She talked like she might have Chris back if he straightened up and put aside his gambling. And even if he doesn't, she has a plan in place for his financial wellbeing."

"That's the problem." Steve shook his head. "It's her plan and not his."

"It's an addiction," said Heather.

"Umm."

"You don't think gambling can be an addiction?"

Steve let out a huff. "It's doesn't matter what I think. All I'm sure of is people mess up their lives and sometimes commit violent crimes because they gambled themselves into trouble."

He motioned for Heather to drive. "Let's talk about the case, the suspects, and what we both learned. You go first and tell me about Dora Chen. I almost swallowed my tongue when you asked Melody if she knew Dora was an optometrist in South Korea."

Heather waited for a break in the traffic to leave the parking lot. Once on the way to Chris's retail store, she began her report. "My source said Dora was a top student who had a successful practice before she came to the States. No criminal record. She married a US serviceman and followed him to Texas. That's where the story gets muddy. I have a call in to find out about his service record. From what I've learned so far, he was more of a ball and chain to her than a decent husband."

"Hmm," said Steve. "We need to find out if she's trying to get her license to practice here. Also, see if you can discover if she's been in contact with anyone from Dr. Raymond Lee's organization."

Something clicked in Heather's mind. "Do you think Dora might angle to work for Dr. Lee?"

Steve shrugged. "It's worth considering. She's the assistant in Melody's clinic. If she's on the verge of getting her license to practice optometry, she might have designs on a potential fast track to success."

Heather wheeled a left turn and entered the onramp to I-45. "There's two big assumptions in that theory."

"More than that," said Steve. "But all the pieces could fit together."

They drove for a couple of miles in silence. Heather broke it with a question. "What about Cindy Green, the evening sales clerk in Dr. Melody's store? She could have known that the Lee family was interested in taking over the store, along with the practice."

Steve pulled the seat belt away from his chest an inch or two. "You might as well include Bryson Wayne if you're looking at people with a key to Melody's store. They both have access to the file cabinet."

Heather shook her head. "I'm having a hard time picturing either of them killing Cleo Stanley."

Steve allowed the seat belt to retract against his chest. "The only motive I can think of is a quick buck for providing the tax returns to Dr. Lee. I'll have Detective Hall get into their bank accounts and see if they've had any recent financial windfalls."

Heather cut her eyes to see Steve. "You're giving Hall busy work. Those two are at the bottom of your list of suspects."

He grinned. "If you'd rather do it, it's all yours."

"No thanks. The names I heard this morning are Dr. Raymond Lee and his son. I'll focus on them this afternoon."

"It may take more time than that," said Steve. "He has a large family and any of them could have approached our suspects."

Steve then veered off the path of talking about the case. "Tell me about your trip to Boston."

Heather gripped the steering wheel. "Have you spoken with Jack about it?"

"He called, but didn't go into detail. I understand he and your father had a private meeting."

Heather tightened her grip. "I should have gone in with him. I know how to deal with Father."

"Jack also said you two stayed up late to make phone calls to South Korea."

"And finished the research on the business side of optometry and selling eyeglasses. It was a full day and night."

"Yeah, I bet." He chuckled. "When Maggie and I were in

college, we'd call our late-night study session in my car 'extended library hours.'"

Heather let out a huff. "There has to be Puritan blood running through Father's veins instead of Scotch-Irish. He used our midnight rendezvous as a reason to send Jack packing." She looked down at her fingertips, white from the grip on the wheel. "I was so proud of Jack for telling Father what he could do with the airplane ticket he bought."

Steve turned toward her. "Your father actually bought an airline ticket for Jack?"

"He delivered it at breakfast and made it abundantly clear that Jack wasn't welcome to stay any longer."

"That doesn't sound like your father."

"You don't know him like I do." Her voice hardened. "He likes things his way. Can you believe he thinks I'll come back to Boston? Then he'd choose a husband for me with the proper pedigree and portfolio."

She looked straight ahead and spoke to herself as much as to Steve. "This time Father is sorely mistaken. After hurricane season, I'm shopping for a very special item."

The rest of the trip to Chris's office passed without talking until Heather pulled into the parking lot. "We're here. I hope you have questions ready for Sandi. My life reminds me of a Jenga game that came crashing down. I'm not sure I can think straight until I put it back together."

"You'll rebuild your life higher than you ever thought possible."

Heather shook her head. "I appreciate your optimism, but when I looked in the mirror this morning, I saw Humpty Dumpty."

Steve moved his hand to the door latch. "There's nothing like solving a case to help put the pieces back together. Let's find out what Sandi knows about keys to Melody's store."

Heather leaned into Steve and whispered as the door to Chris's eyeglass store closed behind them. "Sandi's fitting one customer for glasses and has four more waiting."

"I'm in no rush. Does anything look different in here?"

Heather scanned the oversized room. "Another employee is coming out of the back room. We may not have to wait as long as I thought."

Steve placed both hands on the top of his cane. "Five customers at a time isn't bad."

"Five?"

"Your reading glasses should have arrived."

"I forgot all about them."

Sandi greeted them from across the room. "Hello, Ms. McBlythe. Your glasses came in yesterday afternoon. I'll be with you as soon as I can."

Heather turned to Steve. "Do you want to try on sunglasses while we're waiting?"

"Do I need to?"

"I thought you might like a change. Those have a tendency to slide down your nose."

Steve shrugged. "They'll be cheaper at other stores. Perhaps Kate could go with us to pick out a new pair."

Heather pulled away an inch or two. "Don't you trust me?"

"It's not that I don't trust you. Kate and I are the same age. We speak the same language when it comes to style."

Heather spurted out a laugh. "Who are you trying to kid? Your favorite place to shop is Goodwill."

"That's what I mean. Kate told me she finds all kinds of decent clothes there. Do you know if they sell sunglasses?"

"You want used sunglasses?"

Steve huffed. "Goodwill sells both used and new items. How long has it been since you shopped there?"

"I hit the second-hand stores hard during the lean years as a cop."

"And now your personal assistant picks out your clothes for you."

Heather tented her hands on her hips. "It makes little sense for me to spend a half day shopping when I can—"

"Add to your portfolio?"

She took a long look at Steve. Something about this conversation grated on her. Was he pressing her buttons on purpose? Kidding banter was their stock-in-trade, but this went deeper. Was it mild criticism? Probably not, but what was it? Then it came to her. Steve was afraid. His feelings for Kate went deeper than he let on. He wanted to hang on to Maggie's memories, but time has a way of fading them. He'd mentioned his desire for Kate to help him make a selection with sunglasses. Was he ready for her to share his dark world?

Heather made a tactical retreat. "You're right. Kate's closer to your age than me. I'm likely to have you in leopard-print frames with dark blue lenses."

"More likely, mirrored aviator sunglasses. All the young women would think an old pervert was checking them out."

They made a slow trip around the perimeter of the store and wound up at Sandi Fields's work station as she finished with a customer. The young man left with a smile of satisfaction on his face. Heather wondered if it was because he thought the glasses made him look smarter, or because Sandi had told him how women went for men in glasses with frames that communicated power and affluence.

Sandi collected her paperwork, stood, and said, "Take a seat at the center work station. I'll get your glasses and make any final adjustments they may need."

Heather led Steve and settled him in the chair next to her. "You remember Steve, don't you?"

"Of course. How are you Mr. Smiley? I saw Heather looking at our selection of men's sunglasses and noticed how yours have a tendency to slide down your nose. If you like, I can fit you with something that will make you look five years younger."

"That's the same thing a vitamin supplement salesman said on television. Could you adjust these instead?"

Sandi leaned across the table, wasted showing cleavage to a blind man, and said, "I'm not supposed to adjust glasses that weren't purchased here, but I won't tell anyone if you don't."

Steve made an X over the left side of his chest with his right hand. "I cross my heart and hope to die if I squeal on you."

Sandi leaned back and pulled up the zipper on the medical-looking smock. Heather guessed one reason for Sandi's success had to do with giving a show to the male customers who came in without a wife or girlfriend.

"Do you want me to take off my sunglasses?" asked Steve.

"I'll get them after I see if they're sitting crooked."

After a visual inspection of the earpieces, Sandi grasped the glasses on each side, slid them forward, and pushed them back. "The hinges are a little bent on each side. This will be an easy fix." She pulled an unusual-looking pair of pliers from a pocket and went to work bending the glasses back into shape.

While she worked, Steve said, "Since we're here, there's something I wanted to ask you. Do you still have keys to Dr. Melody's retail store?"

"I gave my keys to the store and the file cabinets to Dr. Chris."

"Do you know if he gave them to Dr. Melody?"

"I suppose he did. She sent out a tacky email demanding them back... or else."

"Or else what?" asked Heather.

She shrugged. "Beats me. I sent a curt reply, telling her Chris had them. I never heard from her again."

She took the sunglasses, cleaned the lenses, and slid them back on Steve's head. "How do they feel?"

"Like a new pair. I didn't realize how loose they were."

"Come back if they continue to slide. Eventually, I'll get you into something more sophisticated."

Steve then asked, "It's our understanding that Chris considered selling his practice and eyeglass store before his divorce. Did you know that?"

"Sorry," said Sandi. "I had my head buried in a drawer where we keep newly received glasses and didn't hear you."

"I asked if you knew Chris considered selling his practice and store before he and Melody split."

"Everyone knew. He was excited about it."

"Why was he excited?" asked Heather.

"He said it would put an end to his problems."

Steve asked, "Do you mean his problems caused by gambling?"

Sandi froze in place and then thawed enough to lower her head. "You found out."

"It wasn't hard."

"He does good for two or three weeks, and then something snaps in his brain. I try talking to him about it. He listens and agrees with everything I say. Then he finds a cheap flight to Vegas and he's off again. He'll straighten up for a while, get back on his feet, and work his way out of the holes he dug."

"How far down is he now?"

Sandi lifted her chin. "Have you been to his practice lately? Everything he owns is in one of the exam rooms. They evicted him from his apartment. Right now, he's sleeping on my couch."

"I get the picture," said Steve.

Sandi kept talking without being prompted. "He hides what's going on, but I can tell he's scared to death about what happened to Mattie Arnold." She then regained her composure and went about fitting Heather's glasses.

Heather had one more question as Sandi made adjustments to the earpieces. "Do you know if anyone has approached Chris again about selling his practice and this store?"

"He's been more upbeat lately, so something like that wouldn't surprise me. If it's the same people that tried to buy him out before, I'll need to look for another job. They pay straight salary with no sales bonuses. Where's the incentive to give great service and upsell?"

Heather looked in an oval mirror. "Not as bad as I feared."

"Bad?" said Sandi. "Those give you that little something special that men find adorable."

Heather didn't know if she agreed, but she had to admit squinting at menus wasn't the look she wanted.

They thanked Sandi for her great service and promised to leave a review online. Heather remembered to start the SUV with her key fob and had it cooling as they left the store. Steve nodded his approval as he entered the vehicle. "Much better."

"What's next?" asked Heather.

"Home. We need to verify that Chris is trying to sell his businesses."

"How do we do that?"

Steve adjusted the air vent on his side. "That's up to you, but if it were me, I'd call Chris and tell him you want to put in a bid."

"If my mind wasn't so scattered, I'd have thought of that." Ghostlike figures of Mother, Father, and Jack all paraded across the dashboard and were gone with a blink of her eyes. "What are you going to do while I'm preparing an offer?"

"Lunch, and work on my short story with Kate."

"Good for you," said Heather, and she meant it. Perhaps someday Steve's ability to mix work with rest would rub off on her.

25

———————

With plenty of time before lunch, Steve walked into his condo and settled in his recliner. It wasn't long before he heard the magnetic edges on the cat door give way to Max's push. A short time later, Max let out a deep welcome home meow, leapt onto the couch, and made the quick trip from the arm to Steve's lap. Purrs began with the first stroke across Max's wide head. "I'm glad to be home, buddy. Things are getting interesting and I'm not sure how everything will turn out. I'll either be a hero or a big zero."

Max settled on his lap with his head in the perfect position to receive more strokes.

"Have I told you I appreciate the way you listen? It's good to have another guy around." More strokes. "I need some advice. Do you have any suggestions on how I can tell Kate she needs to go back to Florida?"

More purrs.

"What's that? You don't want her to leave?" He paused and thought. "You're a smart cat and a good friend, but I don't think you understand why she has to go. I'm not sure I understand. All I know is, I'm not ready for anything more than a long-distance friendship, and I don't believe Kate is either. Besides, I don't have time for anything else right now. This case is coming to a close and I need to save my partnership, and friendship, with Heather. She's taken a lot off me in the past but I may have gone too far this time."

Max yawned and settled on his stomach. "You must have already eaten; you're ready for an afternoon nap. If you want to go to my bed, I'll turn the ceiling fan on for you. Kate and Heather should be here soon for lunch."

He pulled on the chair's wooden handle. Max let out a meow of discontent.

"Don't be such a grump. Go back to my bed and take a nap." Faint sounds told Steve Max retraced his path to the couch and down to the living room floor.

If it were a normal day, Steve would turn on the television and listen to the noon news. Not today. With the case nearing its end, he had to go over every scrap of information he or Heather had gathered.

He rubbed his chin and considered how to find the right words to tell Kate to return to her life in Miami. All the speeches he tried came out sounding harsh or apologetic. He sighed, rose from his chair, and walked into the kitchen.

Steve released the handle of the refrigerator door when he heard a knock. "Come in," he shouted.

He could tell by the footsteps that Kate came alone. "Heather's not hungry?"

"She said something about setting a trap for an ophthalmologist, and she needed to call Jack."

Steve chuckled. "That sounds like two traps."

Kate's hand found his arm. "Do you think she suspects anything?"

"Not yet, but we need to keep her off balance until I get the final few bits of information to close out the case."

"How do you propose to do that?"

Steve scratched his left cheek. "You may not like the answer."

She removed her hand. "Give it to me straight."

"What if we staged a disagreement?"

Kate stayed silent for several seconds. "She might see through my horrible acting skills. What if I simply fly back to Florida?"

Steve took a step back. "Have you been talking to Max?"

Out came the laugh he'd miss. "You're the one that carries on conversations with Max. Did you tell him it was time for me to leave?"

"Not in those words, but how did you know?"

"I've read, and written, so many romance novels, I knew how this chapter between us would end. Sometimes life really does imitate art."

"No hard feelings?"

"Are you kidding? This has been the most enjoyable thing I've done in years. My notebook is awash with ideas for characters, plots, and settings. Joining in a real investigation has stimulated me so much that I can't wait to get back to writing full time. What's your plan?"

Steve took a seat at the table. "I'm not skilled at having pretend disagreements with girlfriends. I'll defer to your expertise."

Kate sat opposite him. "Your idea isn't without merit. We could have a public disagreement and make a scene."

Steve shook his head. "That seems out of character for both of us. The last time you got really mad at me, you shut down and didn't accept my apology for several months. Pretend you're writing a similar scene in a book. What else would you have your characters do?"

"A note could work." A trill of excitement filled her words. "In a cryptic paragraph I'll thank Heather for her hospitality, but won't explain my sudden departure. She'll assume we had a fight."

"That's much better. I wouldn't have to deceive her more than I already have." Steve did a drum roll on the top of the table. "I like it. When are you leaving?"

"Let's shoot for the day after tomorrow. I'll check flights for the best prices, and I don't mean for first-class tickets. It was very kind of you, but you wasted a lot of money on airfare and that rental. I'm a cheap-seat kind of woman and have more frequent flier miles than I can count."

"That's being thrifty, not cheap."

Kate rose from her chair. "What kind of sandwich do you want today?"

"I think I'll practice thrift and have a rerun of the pot roast I brought home the other night."

"Good choice. I'll have a salad. Clean up will be a snap."

Kate busied herself and spoke as she worked. "Since I'm leaving before you close the case, are you going to tell me who's responsible for Cleo Stanley's death and the capsaicin in the eye drops?"

"You know a mystery writer can't reveal who done it before completing the investigation."

Kate's laugh filled the kitchen. "If you don't call me after the arrest, I'll come back and we'll have a proper fight."

HEATHER PLACED HER PHONE ON THE TABLE BESIDE THE couch. She eased back into the cushion and thought about how easy it was to get a rumor started. All it took was a few phone calls to people who knew the right people in Dr. Raymond Lee's small empire. Word would quickly spread that a new player proposed to purchase Dr. Christopher Craddock's practice and adjoining retail store.

She considered calling Jack but looked at the clock and realized he had office appointments scheduled and wouldn't be free for another hour. A pang of hunger made her consider rummaging through Steve's refrigerator for lunch, but she decided against it. Steve and Kate were hitting it off, and she didn't want to interfere with a blossoming relationship.

A search of her refrigerator and pantry revealed her choices for lunch were a bowl of whole grain cereal with almond milk or celery stalks. She also found a container of garden vegetable cream cheese spread. Stuffed celery would do.

While taking a third bite, her phone vibrated. Jack's name, number, and smiling face appeared on the screen. "How did you know I was thinking of you?"

His reply brought her upbeat mood to a quick end. "The ambulance is on the way to pick up Mom again."

"Is it her heart?"

"I think so."

"Did you give her a nitro tablet?"

A woman's moan sounded.

Jack answered Heather's question. "The tablet went under her tongue when I saw her grip her chest."

Heather pushed open her bedroom door. "The same hospital?"

"If it isn't, I'll let you know."

Heather activated the phone's speaker and placed it on the bed. While taking a pair of jeans from the closet, she hollered over her shoulder. "I'm on my way."

The phone went dead. She snatched a long sleeve blouse and changed clothes. Remembering the frigid temperature of the waiting room the last time Cora had a spell, she grabbed a summer-weight sweater. Her mind raced through a list of things she needed for another multi-hour stay. She dashed into the bathroom to get a toothbrush and a travel-size tube of toothpaste. "I need two toothbrushes. Money? Yes." She continued talking to herself as she made it to the dining room. "I have plenty of cash left over from the trip to Boston. Phone charger. I really should keep an extra in my SUV."

She stuffed the items in her purse and hollered at the cat door. "I'm coming over." In mere seconds, she threw open Steve's front door without knocking and took two steps inside. Both he and Kate sat at the dining room table.

"It's Cora's heart again. First responders should be there by now."

"Go," said Steve.

Heather's thoughts pinballed as she drove north on I-45 to Conroe. How serious was Cora's condition this time? When was her stress test? Wednesday or Thursday?

She couldn't recall. Perhaps her mother's sudden death clouded her memory. She then spoke out loud, as if hearing the words would bring clarity. "It's no wonder I can't think straight, the way Father treated Jack."

She heaved a deep sigh. "Poor Jack. I've put him through too much." She made another inner vow that as soon as this emergency passed and the case ended, big changes would take place. A sharp nod sealed the deal she made with herself.

The voices in her head kept playing until she pulled into the hospital's parking lot. Cool air swooped down from overhead blowers as glass doors whooshed open. Jack stood in front of the admission clerk's glass window, his back to her. She sidled beside him and put her hand on his back. Worry lines creased the corners of his mouth as he kept answering questions from the woman on the other side of the transparent barrier. Then, he pulled her tight against him and she breathed a sigh of partial relief. This was her new home... next to Jack.

The questions ended, and they looked around the waiting room for two seats together. Once they settled as far away from a television as possible, Jack said, "I think she'll be all right, but you may have a homicide to investigate after this is over."

"Why?"

"My mother, in her infinite wisdom, canceled her stress test and bought a treadmill instead."

Heather sensed her eyes had bugged out. "What was she thinking?"

"That exercise and diet would cure her. She stuck the contraption in the break room at the office and put herself on a daily routine of walking at a fast pace for ten minutes every two hours. This morning, she missed her first three exercise breaks and caught up by doing all three at lunch. I didn't realize what she'd done until she hollered for me."

"Doesn't she realize she isn't getting any younger?"

Jack held up his hands in surrender. "She won't listen to me."

"Do they think it's a heart attack?"

Jack let out a huff through his nose, lifted his shoulders, and let them fall.

"Did she lose consciousness?"

"Never did, but she was hurting, panting, and sweating. She said it was like a thick belt tightened around her chest."

Jack took in a deep breath and let it out with a long, slow blow. He looked at her. "Thanks for coming, my love."

She pulled his arm against her. "This is where I belong."

Jack smiled and then cast his gaze around the room. "Same room, different faces."

Heather looked out at the gathering. "All ages, sizes, and colors. Hospitals and emergency rooms may be the best examples of democracy in the world. Most everyone gets sick or injured at some time."

"And loved ones get to wait."

For the next hour, that's what they did, until a nurse called out Jack's name. He rose and turned to Heather. "Come with me."

"They may not let me in," whispered Heather.

He looked at a ring she wore on her right hand. "Put that on your left ring finger and turn it around so only the band shows."

She did as instructed, looked down, and gave a nod of approval.

The nurse looked as if she had six things to do and not enough time to complete three of them. "Follow me. Dr. Sanchez will speak to you."

"Is Dr. Sanchez the emergency room doctor?" asked Heather.

"She is, and she's swamped. I hope you have your questions

ready." The nurse stopped at a closed door and pushed it open. "Go on in, dear. Your mother-in-law is resting comfortably."

Once inside, they found Cora awake and with something to say. "This is just like the last time. There's nothing wrong with me. I just overdid it today."

Jack shook his head. "Your license to practice medicine is hereby revoked. This time you're going to follow the doctor's instructions."

Heather took the hand that didn't have an IV tube snaking away from it. Before she could say anything to Cora, the door flew open.

"I'm Dr. Sanchez. Sorry to keep you waiting. Normally I'd leave your mother here until I had all the test results before I admitted her, but with the ER at capacity today that's not possible. I spoke with the EMTs and her cardiologist. They both told me she was supposed to have a stress test but canceled it. Now she's had an exercise-induced heart attack because she pretended to be twenty-five again."

The doctor barely took a breath. "Her cardiologist and I agree we have two options. I can admit her to the cardiac wing upstairs, where she'll stay until we complete all tests and procedures. That will probably take several days. Of course, if she needs surgery her stay would be longer."

She paused for effect.

"She can also refuse treatment. If she does, I'll release her and you can find another hospital or take her home and hope for the best."

Heather and Jack spoke over each other. She said, "I think it's best she goes to the cardiac wing." Jack said, "She stays here."

The doctor looked at Cora, her eyebrows raised in question. "Do you concur Mrs. Blackstock?"

Cora sighed. "I'll stay."

The doctor gave a firm nod and turned back to Jack. "She's stable and I expect no more surprises unless she runs up and down the stairs."

"We'll tie her to the bed if we have to."

They returned to the lobby and found Steve and Kate sitting in the chairs she and Jack abandoned. Heather wondered how she'd be able to keep working on the case and be with Jack and Cora at the same time. It was only a passing thought, but one she'd need to talk to Steve about.

26

———

"Would you mind finding a trash can for this? I've been holding it for twenty minutes." Steve handed Kate the empty coffee cup he'd drained and prepared to leave the emergency room. Fingers touched and the cup slid from his grip. "How long have we been here?"

"Three hours. It took that long to transfer her upstairs. It was good to see Heather and Jack together. They make a lovely couple." She giggled. "Thanks to your sneaky manipulation."

"I prefer to call it strategic guidance, and don't pop the cork on a bottle of champagne yet. She's a tough nut to crack and the wheels can fly off at any time."

They kept walking across the hospital's parking lot. "You and Heather were gone for almost an hour getting coffee. What took you so long?"

"We went over the details of the case and concluded we're one answer short of being able to call Detective Hall and turn our results over to him."

"By results, do you mean the person responsible for Cleo Stanley's death?"

"Uh-huh, but there's also the matter of the hot pepper juice in the eye drops."

They made it to the rental and Kate delivered him to the passenger side door. Once inside, with the air conditioner blowing, Steve asked, "What time is it?"

"Almost six in the evening."

"No wonder I'm hungry. How would you like a slab of barbecue ribs?"

"It wouldn't be a trip to Texas without barbecue."

"There's an out-of-the-way place going to Lake Conroe with ribs so tender I can't promise there'll be any leftovers to take home."

Kate spoke after they both settled into the rental. "With your love of leftovers, we'll have to get a couple of pounds to go."

"I like the way you think."

"What's the name of this place? I'll put it on the computer and that cute Australian voice will tell us how to get there."

"Bill's Texas Smoke Shack."

Kate worked her magic on the onboard navigation system, and before long they were on their way to barbecue nirvana.

Steve put his head back against the leather headrest. He and Heather had their plan now on wrapping up the case. The only thing missing would be Heather if she needed to stay with Jack and Cora. He ran a scenario through his mind of how he'd conduct the meeting with all the suspects, but without her. The possibility didn't appeal to him. She picked up on so much that he couldn't, and the end of an investigation wasn't the time to miss something that could turn the case upside down.

"You've gone silent," said Kate. "Something on your mind?"

"I was thinking about how to close the case without Heather. I've grown accustomed to relying on her to catch last-minute surprises."

A few seconds of silence followed. "I'm a poor substitute for Heather, but I could stay on if you need me to."

Steve cleared his throat to buy an extra second or two before he answered. "She's never missed us closing a case together. I'm betting on her doing whatever is necessary to be there."

"Don't you think Jack and Cora need her more?"

"Heather's one of those rare people who can immerse herself in multiple things at the same time and do them all well. She'll be there."

"And if she's not?"

"Then I lose the bet."

"Who did you bet with?"

"Myself, and I always pay if I lose. The money goes from one pocket to the other."

Kate laughed, which gave Steve time to come up with a serious follow-up line. "If only Chris would have learned that trick."

Kate's voice changed to match the lament in his. "How often do you think or say, 'If only?'"

"Not as often as I used to, but it's like a favorite song from college that gets stuck in my head."

Steve straightened his posture and put a more hopeful tone to his voice. "We must be close. I can smell the smoke from the barbecue pit."

Kate's hand rested on his arm. "We're at least ten miles from the restaurant. You can relax. I'll not ask again if you want me to stay." She turned on the radio and searched stations until she found one playing classic country. "We need music to fit the mood of Bill's Texas Smoke Shack."

The opening riff of a long-ago song caused Steve to moan. "Now you've done it. That song will stick in my head for the next week."

Disoriented to time, Steve awoke with Max's front paws putting divots in his chest and a serenade of insistent meows. He slapped at a clock on the nightstand and a mechanical voice replied, "Monday, August twenty, 9:30 a.m."

Max continued to express his displeasure while Steve said,

"Sorry, buddy. It was another one of those nights where I couldn't slow my mind down. Too many things going on." He held out his hand and Max stopped the kneading of his paws, nudged the hand with his nose, and received a good scratch.

"Okay, buddy. Time to get up." Steve slipped out of bed and prepared to meet the day with Max making laps around his ankles.

"I hope Kate didn't wait until I got up for breakfast. Did she feed you?"

Max's only response was a yawn.

"Yeah, she must have fed you. Otherwise, you wouldn't have let me sleep so long."

Steve checked his phone for texts and voice messages. Two awaited him. The phone sounded like a robot. "First voice message, 2:03 a.m. 'It's Heather. I'm staying the night with Cora. She's asleep. I thought I'd never talk Jack into going home for a few hours. He'll spell me tomorrow so I can come home long enough to shower. Sorry to abandon you with the case so close to ending. It's a good thing Kate's there to help you.'"

The mechanical voice spoke again, "Second voice message, 8:14 a.m. 'Good morning, sleepyhead. I loved your idea about leaving a note telling Heather I'm gone. In fact, it appealed to me so much I thought it best to do it twice. Consider this your thank you and goodbye note. This past week ranks in the top five of my life. I'm calling from the airport. If you sleep past nine, I'll be somewhere over the Gulf of Mexico. If you ever come to Miami again, bring ribs from Bill's.'"

Max let out a long, mournful sound that Steve wasn't sure he'd heard before. "I know, Max, but it's more complicated than you realize."

Steve took three steps down the hall and came to a stop. "Listen, Max. Do you hear water running next door? That means Heather's home. Go check on her."

Max trotted off and soon the pet door resealed behind him.

Steve knew it didn't take long for Heather to shower, throw

on clean clothes, and be out the door, as long as she didn't wash her hair. Today, the faint sound of a hair dryer caught his attention.

The night before, he'd gorged himself on ribs with all the trimmings, so he scaled back on breakfast. A bagel smeared with cream cheese, and coffee would suffice. He pulled out the toaster, plugged it in, prepared his light breakfast, and had Heather's bagel out and ready to toast.

When he heard her talking to Max, he shouted at the pet door. "Coffee and bagel are at Smiley's diner."

"On my way. Can I get them to go?"

"Sure."

In no time, Heather entered the condo with an accusatory question leading the way. "What did you say to Kate to make her leave?"

"Did she leave you a message on your phone, too?"

"Mine's written on a page torn from her notebook, and you didn't answer my question."

"She has her life, I have mine, and you have yours. It's as simple as that."

Heather let out a huff. "I know you too well. Things are never simple."

Steve hated bending the truth, but it was for Heather's good. "All I know is, we went to Bill's last night, stuffed ourselves with ribs, and listened to a cover band play old music."

As if the first huff of disgust wasn't loud enough, Heather made the second one louder. "You know how ribs and old music bring back too many memories for you. You purposefully torpedoed a perfectly good relationship."

Steve shrugged. "Do you want your bagel toasted?"

"And now you're lost in the past. You won't be able to think about the case for days."

"So what?" he said with a snap of his voice. "We have to wait until you hear something from your source before we can call everyone together. What difference does it make what I think about?"

Heather stomped her foot. "You can be so aggravating. I don't have time to discuss this any longer. If you want to die a lonely old man, be my guest."

The next sound Steve heard was the front door slamming shut.

The cat door opened and resealed. "Hey, Max. I guess you heard everything?"

No answer.

"Keep your claws crossed that she doesn't find out." Steve pulled his phone out of the pocket of his shorts. "I'd better call Heather's father and let him know our plan is still on track."

27

———

Three nights later, Heather opened the door to Melody's eyeglass store as Cindy Green, the unofficial assistant manager, turned off the open sign. Cindy asked, "Do you know what's going on? That cute police detective took my keys and wouldn't tell me why."

Heather tilted her head. "What did he say?"

"He told me to go next door and wait at Dr. Melody's practice."

"Then that's what you should do." Her words came out with more bite than Cindy deserved. The dust-up with Steve and long hours at the hospital had put her in a funk.

Heather walked into the room where Cleo Stanley had died. As usual, Steve had a way of knowing she'd arrived.

"There you are. How's Cora?"

"She's back in her room and wants to go home. They thought it would only require one stent, but two of the arteries supplying blood to her heart were ninety percent blocked. The cardiologist said it should make a new woman out of her."

"That's great. How are you and Jack holding up?"

"After sleeping three nights in a hospital recliner, I'm ready for my bed. Jack's puffy eyes make him look like a raccoon, but he's holding up. He'll be here any minute. His brother is taking a turn with Cora."

"Do you have questions about how we're going to handle this?"

Heather shook her head. "The same way we usually do, only this time, all the action will take place in the waiting room of an optometrist's office."

Detective Hall came through the front door and made his way to the center work station. "Everyone's next door. Are you sure I don't need another officer or two?"

"One officer in the parking lot is all we'll need this time."

"I hope you both get a nice long break before I need you again."

"A break would be nice, but I'm not taking any bets," said Heather. "Homicides seem to find Steve three or four times a year. Lucky for you, they don't always happen in your jurisdiction."

Heather turned after hearing the front door to the shop open.

"Hello, Jack," said Steve as Heather walked to meet him. "Let's go next door."

Inside Melody's practice, Jack pointed to the only pair of open chairs. He whispered in Heather's ear, "I'm beat. Can we sit down for this one?"

Heather slid into the first chair to Hall's left, with Jack by her side.

Steve and Detective Hall stood side by side, their backs to the front door. Hall spoke first. "We have two crimes to talk about tonight: the contamination of eye drops, and the death of Cleo Stanley. Mr. Smiley and Ms. McBlythe have been helping with these two investigations and have come to some interesting conclusions. Since they did most of the heavy lifting, I'll let them explain."

Steve handed his cane to Detective Hall, who gave it to

Heather. "Before I begin, I'd like everyone to say their name, so I'll know where you're sitting. Let's go clockwise."

They'd arranged chairs in a semi-circle, giving each person a view of everyone's facial expressions and body language. Heather started things off. "I believe everyone knows I'm Heather McBlythe, Mr. Smiley's partner."

Jack spoke next. "I'm Jack Blackstock, attorney representing Dr. Chris Craddock."

Chris sat next to Jack. "Everyone knows me and Steve knows my voice. I hired Jack to look after both me and Melody."

Heather knew the use of the word *hired* usually meant some sort of remuneration for services rendered, not the pro bono deal he'd wrangled out of Jack.

"I'm Sandi Fields and I manage Dr. Chris's retail store."

"My name is Dora Chen and I work with Dr. Melody Craddock."

"Bryson Wayne, the sales manager for Dr. Melody's store next door."

"Dr. Melody Craddock."

The person in the last seat raised her hand. "I'm Cindy Green, the closing manager for Dr. Melody's retail store."

Bryson spoke up. "No, you're not. Your job title is sales associate."

"Not anymore," said Cindy, with a strut in her voice.

Dr. Melody turned to Bryson. "I made it official today after it came to my attention that Cindy performs the same tasks as you, and the second shift serves a higher volume of customers. If you want to discuss this further, we'll do so after the meeting."

Bryson responded with a scowl and tightly crossed arms and legs.

Steve plowed on, ignoring Bryson's obvious offense. "I found these two cases interesting because the longer we investigated, the more they came together. Two crimes, two locations, two victims, and nothing to link them except the last name of the two optometrists. Or so we thought."

Steve moved only his head to face Dr. Melody. "Did you donate supplies to Chris when he opened his practice after the divorce?"

"I gave him enough to help get his practice started."

"Why was that?"

She shifted in her chair. "You know why, and so does everyone here. He couldn't afford the upfront cost of supplies after he'd borrowed all the money he could for leases, remodeling, and equipment."

"Could the contaminated drops that injured one of his patients have come from your office?"

Melody straightened her spine. "Are you accusing me?"

Steve raised both palms. "I'm playing the part of Chris's defense attorney if this case goes to trial." Steve turned his head. "Is that right, Jack?"

He nodded. "Any defense attorney worth his salt would ask that same question."

Dr. Chris spoke up. "Melody would never do anything like that."

Steve kept his words smooth and even. "I didn't say she did or even imply that Melody had any part in it. I only asked if it was possible the tainted drops came from her practice. The answer is yes. In fact, we know they did. Detective Hall will explain."

Hall gave his head a nod and spoke loud enough for all to hear. "The lot number on the bottle matched the invoice to a delivery made to Dr. Melody's office. From there, it went to Dr. Chris's practice."

Steve took over. "All I wanted to show by asking the question about donated supplies was that there's a link between the two clinics."

Dr. Melody added, "That doesn't negate the possibility the tampering took place at the factory or anywhere along the supply chain."

"True," said Steve. "That's why we shifted our investigation from means to opportunity and motive. Was this an attack on a particular person, or random? A thorough check of Mattie Arnold's background showed no reason to believe anyone singled her out as the target. If this wasn't against Mattie, then why?"

"It was against me," said Chris. He dipped his head. "I meant to say against my practice."

"Give me a motive," said Steve.

Chris shrugged. "Beats me. I wrote it off to bad luck, not some grand conspiracy."

Steve's top lip gave a slight upward tug. "Let's stay on motive a while longer. The motive for a crime almost always has something to do with money, anger, or revenge."

The air conditioner cycled off, giving further clarity to Steve's words. "It made little sense to us that Chris would sabotage his own business. Child support and loan repayments would end for Melody if Chris's business tanked, so she didn't seem a likely suspect. Nor did Cindy Green or Bryson Wayne."

Steve paused, took in a deep breath, and said, "That brings us to Sandi Fields." He let the name linger in the air.

Sandi's voice rose to emphasize her firm denial. "Don't look at me. All I do is sell glasses and contacts. I wouldn't know one bottle of eye drops from another and I rarely go to Chris's office."

"Be that as it may," said Steve. "You did all you could to conceal the truth."

"That's not true."

Steve tilted his head. "Did you leave your job as manager of what is now Dr. Melody's retail store to follow Chris?"

She paused a moment too long. "I thought it might have better long-term potential."

"Did you have an affair with Chris?"

"That's none of your business."

"Chris already told us about it. Did you go on the cruise in the spring that Chris went on?"

"So what?"

"Did you share a cabin with him?"

"No. He and some friends had a crazy bet about who could save the most money and they slept two to a room in inexpensive cabins."

"How did he win the bet?"

"Ask Chris."

"We did. He lied."

"Now, wait a minute," said Chris.

Steve carried on speaking to Sandi as if Chris hadn't interrupted. "You spent time with him on the ship, didn't you?"

"We bumped into each other from time to time."

"Where?" Steve pointed at her. "Don't lie about this one. I already know the answer."

Sandi lifted her chin in what looked like an act of defiance. "We met in the casino. He called me his lady luck, and perhaps I was this time. He hit a hot streak."

Jack piped up. "You said you won prizes playing trivia, taking part in dance classes, and doing the things the rest of us didn't want to do."

Chris shot back, "I paid you back for the cruise, didn't I? What did it matter where the money came from?"

Steve took a step toward Chris and lowered his voice. "Where are you sleeping these days?"

Chris's face took on a pinkish tone. "Sometimes in an exam room at my practice."

"Sandi said you stay at her apartment."

"On the couch," added Sandi.

Bryson let out a snort, followed by, "Good luck selling that fairy tale."

Steve pressed on. "Chris's luck didn't last long, did it, Sandi?"

Heather watched as Sandi's chin quivered. "I told him he had to leave, but he talked me into letting him stay. I'm trying to help him change, but everything I do backfires because of his gambling."

Melody stared at Chris. "Where do our children stay on the weekends you take them?"

"We go to Mom and Dad's."

"That's a five-hour drive from here, and it's near the Oklahoma border." She pointed an accusatory finger. "You're dropping them off at your parents and going to the casinos."

Chris didn't deny it, so Steve took a step back and allowed the words to have their full effect.

Heather watched the faces of all those assembled. They appeared to be a mixture of pity and condemnation.

Steve broke the silence by saying, "Before the rest of you are tempted to think you're without fault, let's consider some other things that make these cases interesting."

28

"Melody," said Steve. "Have you studied much about gambling addiction?"

Heather focused on Melody's reaction. She dipped her head and worried a fingernail. Then she looked up and spoke in a firm voice. "I read every book and article on it I can find. I also go to a support group for family and friends of compulsive gamblers."

"Give me the short version of what the research says about co-dependency."

Melody took in a deep breath. "Studies show that family and friends should allow compulsive gamblers to suffer the consequences of their actions, especially if the gambler is in denial. We're not to do anything to enable their addiction."

Steve swiveled his head. "Chris, do you have a gambling problem?"

"Absolutely not."

The responses of those gathered told a different story. Everything from mumbles to laughter rang out.

Steve said, "It seems I'm not the only blind person in the room."

Turning back to face Melody, Steve said, "You did nothing illegal, but your generosity in stocking Chris's practice set up a chain of events that no one could have predicted. You must have known he'd eventually gamble away his businesses, yet you gave him supplies to make sure he could open."

A tear slid down Melody's cheek. "I know, but he has to make a living."

Steve's next words came out sounding like the bark of a Doberman. "No! He gambles everything away, and you know it." He dragged his right hand down his face and took the intensity out of his next words. "Your intentions were noble, but you knew better, didn't you?"

Melody squared her shoulders. "It won't happen again."

"I hope not, because you're likely to be tested."

"What's that supposed to mean?" asked Chris.

"I'll get to you after Heather deals with the person I haven't mentioned yet. Ms. McBlythe will take over."

Heather stood and joined Steve and Detective Hall. She turned to Dr. Chris. "Do you know that Dora Chen is a licensed optometrist?"

Chris's eyes and mouth opened wide. He soon composed himself. "Why isn't she practicing? She could make so much more than she is now."

Heather turned to Dora. "I contacted a friend in South Korea. He speaks highly of you. Tell us why you chose not to get your license to practice optometry until recently."

Dora sat as she always did, with perfect posture. Nothing moved but her lips and eyelashes as she blinked every two seconds. "I wanted to acclimate myself to America and learn how a successful business ran here. By hiring on as an assistant, I learned your ways of doing things without the risk of making avoidable mistakes."

"Are you saying it was a strategic decision to take a lower-paying job?"

"Yes."

"Is that the only reason?"

"That is the primary reason."

"What were the other reasons?"

"They are personal."

Heather nodded. "Personal? Are you talking about your husband?"

"Yes."

"Could you elaborate?"

"I choose not to."

Detective Hall took a step forward, but Heather held out her hand to stop him. "Not yet," she whispered. Luckily, the air conditioner had cycled on and her instruction didn't carry to those assembled.

"I understand your reluctance to talk about uncomfortable personal issues, and I can't force you to. However, we're assisting the police in discovering the truth about why a college student, Mattie Arnold, is the victim of an assault. We also need to discover how and why Cleo Stanley died. To do that, we dove deep into the background of everyone who might be responsible for either of the incidents."

Heather took slow, halting steps toward Melody, but kept her gaze on Dora. "My source in South Korea told me you were a very good optometrist with an eye for detail. No pun intended." She paused. "Dr. Melody and Dr. Chris also speak highly of your work."

No reaction.

"You made excellent grades all your life, but you socialized very little." Heather glanced at Jack. "Believe me, I know what it's like to dedicate yourself to your studies and work." Her gaze and position shifted as she moved to stand directly in front of Dora, leaned over and whispered loud enough for everyone to hear. "It's rewarding in some ways, but lonely. Once you've achieved your life's goals, you want something more."

Heather looked into Dora's dark eyes. "Do you know what I mean?"

The blinking slowed, but Dora still didn't respond with words.

Heather resumed her slow pacing, keeping her gaze trained on the reluctant optometrist. "There you were in Seoul. You had a need to fill, but didn't know what it was. Then you met a man, an American soldier, who opened up a new world to you. You went out. Partied. Had fun. He spoke of what life could be like in America with him and you fell in love with a dream. Perhaps you loved the dream more than the man."

Dora squirmed in her seat.

"Before you knew what was happening, he asked you to come away with him and live in this dream. For the first time in your life, you threw caution to the wind. Leaving everything, you came here where the dream turned sour. His drinking got worse when he left the discipline of military service. He spiraled ever downward into a bottle."

Dora lifted her chin. "You have done much research. I commend you."

Heather stopped walking and stood in front of Dora again. "Now we come to where you took stock and started thinking strategically again. It's I who commend you for gathering your wits before you lost everything. Tell me, what's the first thing you did to protect yourself from being wiped out financially?"

"I went to an attorney who was also a CPA. She told me how to structure my remaining assets before I filed for divorce in such a way my abusive husband would get nothing."

"That was very astute on your part. Were you working for Dr. Melody and Dr. Chris at the time?"

"Yes. It was Dr. Chris who hired me, even though their divorce was imminent. My attorney suggested I delay telling anyone I was getting my license to practice optometry until after my divorce. She said if it went to trial, sympathy might shift from me to my husband."

"You thought this out carefully, didn't you?"

"I followed my attorney's advice."

Heather broke eye contact with Dora and turned her gaze to Chris. "Did Dora know you tried to sell the practice and the eyeglass store to Dr. Lee, but Melody blocked you from doing so?"

"Everyone knew after Melody threw a fit in the hallway. I'd never seen her so mad."

Melody bristled. "You deserved every word. I'm the one who kept this place alive by opening the store next door and keeping that money out of your hands. I had to divorce you before you destroyed everything."

Heather needed to get the conversation back on track, so she asked, "Dora, when did you first contact Dr. Lee?"

Dora's eyelashes fluttered, and she began to cough.

"That won't work. There's no avoiding the question." said Heather. "I spoke with Dr. Lee. He told me you met with him about future employment as an optometrist."

"I choose not to answer your question."

Heather went to stand in front of Dora again. "Up to that point, you'd done nothing terribly illegal, nothing we can prove." She opened her arms out wide. "But that changed when you learned Dr. Chris wanted to sell his current practice and the retail store to Dr. Lee. Then, a new idea came to you. Why work for someone else? You saw how successful Dr. Melody is and you wanted to duplicate her business models. All you needed was Dr. Chris out of the way."

"You can prove nothing."

Heather kept talking, but at a faster pace while keeping her gaze fixed on Dora. "Dr. Chris," said Heather. "Who brought you the last shipment of supplies you received from Melody?"

"Uhh... I don't remember."

"Did you log everything in?"

"Sure. Detective Hall came and rechecked the log today."

Heather turned to the detective. "And what did you find?"

"The log stated Ms. Chen made the delivery the day before the Mattie Arnold incident."

Heather jerked her gaze toward Chris. "Did Dora put supplies in your exam rooms?"

"Now that you mention it, yes. Since I don't have an assistant, she offered to refill any stock in the exam rooms that was low. I thought she was being helpful."

Heather took a step closer to Dora. "You had almost enough money to buy Chris out if you could make him desperate to sell. You believed Dr. Lee was waiting to scoop up a bargain, and you didn't want to get in a bidding war with him. You had to act, so you injected a carefully measured dose of juice from a hot pepper into the bottle of drops used to dilate eyes, knowing it would do no permanent damage. Then, you placed the tainted drops behind an almost empty bottle, knowing Dr. Chris would administer the drops within days."

Dora sat with chin up.

Heather added a few more verbal blows. "Dr. Melody confirmed in a written statement to Detective Hall that she authorized one final shipment of supplies to Dr. Chris within the last two weeks. Those supplies included dilation drops. The written log includes the stock number of the tainted bottle and Dr. Chris's log verifies you delivered them. Finally, we know the press received a tip that something had taken place at Dr. Chris's office that was newsworthy, and you took the day off. Are you sure you were home all day? Or were you in the parking lot watching for activity? The call came from a woman with an accent like yours, but she refused to give details other than the name of Chris's practice and the address."

"Any of his patients or staff could have called."

"They could have, but they didn't."

"Why would I do that?"

"To drive the price down on Dr. Chris's business so you could pay cash for it and the retail business."

Melody spoke up. "She's obsessive-compulsive when it comes to money and believes all debt is not only foolish but evil."

Heather didn't respond to the comment, but turned to Detective Hall. "Your turn."

"I subpoenaed your phone records Ms. Chen. They show you

placed a call to a Houston television station on the morning Mattie Arnold was injured."

Dora leaned forward. "I've studied how your legal system works. If you arrest me, a skilled attorney will have me out on bond, and will drag the case out for more than a year. Eventually, when enough money changes hands, any charges will go away."

Steve stepped forward. "I wouldn't bet on it. One thing's for sure—you'll leave this room in handcuffs. You can also count on a civil suit from Mattie's parents. Lawyers will feed on the bankroll you brought from South Korea like vultures."

Heather added, "Texas law is very clear when it comes to professional standards for optometrists. You'll lose your license. Given the totality of the evidence against you, don't count on ever getting it back."

Dora huffed and muttered, "We shall see."

Steve cleared his throat. "That's one mystery solved, but we're not finished yet. We still need to discuss the death of Cleo Stanley." He motioned with his hand in Chris's direction. "Dr. Chris. I believe you know more about what happened than you've told us."

Jack stood. "Hold on, Steve. It's been a while since I've spoken to my client alone. I'll need a few minutes with Chris to make sure he and I are on the same page."

Steve nodded. "Dr. Melody, would it be all right if Jack and Chris use your office?"

"The door's unlocked."

Detective Hall said, "Everyone else can stand and stretch, but no one is to leave. I'll stay right here to make sure."

29

______

Five minutes later, Heather watched as everyone moved to their original seats. Once the noise of people getting resettled subsided, Steve took center stage. "Near the beginning of this case, Dr. Melody said something about Dr. Chris that caught my attention. She said her ex-husband wasn't to be believed. That reminded me to verify everything anyone said. As you've already heard from several people, Dr. Chris practices not only optometry, but deceit, deception, and outright lies. He's lied for so long to cover his gambling addiction that I'm not sure he knows or cares what the truth is. In a little while, I'll test him to see."

"That's enough," said Chris. "I'm the one who hired you and I can fire you just as easy."

"If you're firing us, then pay us right now. That's the terms of the contract you signed."

Chris crossed his arms and settled back in his chair.

Heather added. "I should note that Dr. Chris isn't the only liar in this room."

Several people shifted in their seat, but didn't respond.

Steve carried on in an even voice. "Let's go back to Dora Chen and see what she thinks of Dr. Chris."

Dora blinked at a normal pace. "He'll do anything to gamble."

Steve gave his head a firm nod. "And to gamble, he has to have money."

"Of course."

"And his latest scheme to get money was to sell his practice to the ophthalmologist, Dr. Raymond Lee. Is that right?"

"I wouldn't know about that."

"I'm going to ask you again, have you ever met or spoken with Dr. Raymond Lee?"

Heather noticed the pace of Dora's blinking slowed.

"I don't think so," said Dora with too much hesitation in her voice.

Steve didn't ask for clarification, but moved on. "Do you have access to the keys for the store next door?"

"I don't work retail."

"I understand, but isn't there a key safe in Dr. Melody's office?"

"There may be, but I don't have a key to it."

"Are you saying you didn't have a key to the business next door on the night Cleo died?"

"That's correct."

Have you ever been in the store next door when it was closed?"

"Yes."

"When was the last time?"

"I went a long time ago, before Dr. Chris and Dr. Melody divorced."

"Why did you need to go there?"

"To repair my glasses."

"How did you get in? Did you have a key then?"

"No. I went over there before work and the manager let me in."

"Were there any other times you went next door apart from normal business hours?"

"Not that I can remember."

He shifted his weight from one foot to the other. "Was it your intention to buy Chris's practice and eyeglass store?"

"That doesn't matter now that you've promised to destroy my way of making a living."

Steve gave a slight bow. "Thank you for your answers." He took in a deep breath and raised his voice. "Now I'll ask Dr. Chris some of the same questions."

"Dr. Chris, did you ever communicate with Dr. Raymond Lee about the possibility of selling your practice to him?"

Chris hiked one leg over the other. "The first time was when Melody and I owned this practice and the store next door." He paused. "Let me correct that. We owned the practice together. The retail store was Melody's project."

"Did you contact Dr. Lee again? Perhaps recently?"

Chris looked at Jack, who gave him the go-ahead with a nod. "Two months ago. I wrote Dr. Lee a letter stating I might sell, provided he guaranteed I could stay on as the optometrist for ten years with an option to renew for another ten."

Dora, who'd been looking straight ahead, jerked her head to the right and cast a withering gaze at Chris.

"What was the response to your offer?" asked Steve.

"Dr. Lee rejected it outright."

"Did Dora know about Dr. Lee's rejection of your proposal?"

Chris shrugged. "I didn't tell her."

"Why did you want to work for someone else?"

Chris looked down at his shoes and then back up. "I wanted to keep providing for my kids. Melody insists the courts garnish what I owe her every month. It's too tempting for me to be in charge of the finances."

Steve made a rolling motion with his hand. "That's not all. Keep talking."

Chris swallowed hard. "I don't do well being self-employed. When it was me and Melody, she tried to keep me out of the casinos and minimized my online gambling. She watched the money as close as she could, but I always found ways to get around her. I'm surprised she put up with me as long as she did."

The words settled. "Between the gambling and my infidelity, it was too much for her. I've concluded I can't make it being my own boss. If I'm on a straight, steady salary and don't have access to most of it, I'll do better."

"Is that when Dora approached you to buy your businesses?"

He nodded and whispered, "Yes."

Steve asked, "Do you have keys to the store next door?"

"No."

"When, and to whom, did you return the keys?"

"Three months ago, I gave them to Sandi Fields and asked her to return them."

Sandi reached in her purse and jangled a shiny set of keys. "I forgot he gave them to me. I've been meaning to give them to Dr. Melody."

Steve shifted his weight. "Sandi, you're a terrible liar. I do wish you'd stop."

Heather added, "We knew you still had them."

Sandy looked at her shoes. "I'm a bit of a scatterbrain. I didn't realize I had them until you jogged my memory tonight." A reddish tint climbed into her face.

"Now you've officially joined the local liars club, but that's all right, we caught on early. You and Chris also stretched the truth about your relationship being a one-off fling. It took some doing, but I tracked down your cabin steward on the cruise you took this past spring. It seems you two *happened* to bump into each other in the casino and also in your cabin."

"See," said Dora. "More lies."

"I have to agree with you on that," said Steve. "Listening to lies is nothing new in our business. The tricky part is to separate out what is and isn't true. Like, who had keys to get in the store on the night Cleo Stanley died?"

Steve scratched his chin. "Isn't it amazing how a simple thing like forgetting to turn in a set of keys can result in the death of good woman?"

Dora pointed at Steve. "I had nothing to do with that cleaning lady's death."

Steve waved away her response. "I didn't say you did. What I know is that you don't have an alibi for the night Cleo died. We've checked everyone else's alibi and they have witnesses for where they were. Only you and two other people can't account for your whereabouts."

"I was home in my apartment... alone," said Dora with emphasis.

"Are you sure you didn't go to Dr. Melody's retail store?"

"You can't prove I was anywhere near that business when Cleo Stanley died."

Steve rubbed his open hand on the back of his neck. "I can if there are two witnesses who saw you there." He faced Sandi. "Where did you say you were on the night Cleo died?"

"I was with Chris," said Sandi.

Chris gave an exaggerated nod. "And I was with Sandi."

"That's an accurate statement. But where were you?"

They spoke over each other that they were in Sandi's apartment.

"That's another correct statement," said Steve. "Let me be even more exact." He held up a hand. "Before you answer, Detective Hall will tell you something that might jog your memory."

Hall took a step forward. "Modern forensic science tells us it's almost impossible for a person to go to a location and not leave evidence. All it takes is a follicle of hair or a smudge of oil you might have walked in. We know who was in that business the night Mrs. Stanley died."

"Now," said Steve as Hall took a step back. "Let's get very specific. Sandi, remember, we already know the answer to this question. Did you go to the eyeglass store next door the night Cleo died?"

Sandi hung her head, nodded, and spoke a weak, "Yes."

"Was Chris with you?"

"Yes."

"What about Dora Chen? Was she also in the store?"

"Uh-huh."

"That's another lie," countered Dora.

Steve turned his head. "What about it, Chris? Are you up to telling the truth? Were you next door with Sandi and Dora the night Cleo Stanley died?"

"Don't answer that," said Jack.

Chris hung his head and then looked up. "I can't stand this any longer. Yes. I was there."

"Did you bring a file folder with you?"

"Yes."

Steve increased his volume. "Dora's a stickler for details and wanted to have accurate, up-to-date numbers on the profitability of Melody's retail store."

Chris added, "I wanted to appease her and keep her on track to buy me out. I offered to get the records for her."

Steve picked up where he left off. "You weren't satisfied with making a fair profit. You wanted more, so you made up a false file exaggerating Melody's profits and switched the files at the last moment."

Heather spoke for the first time in a while. "It's the old story of two thieves trying to outfox each other. Dora, you had enough money to buy him out, as long as it was at your price. But you're a planner. You didn't want to take a chance. You needed that profit-and-loss statement."

Steve took over. "Dora tried to stack the deck in her favor by contaminating eye drops to damage Chris's reputation, thus making him desperate to sell."

Bryson Wayne, the co-manager of the store next door, sat with eyebrows pinched together. "Unless I missed something, you still haven't addressed the biggest question. Who killed Cleo Stanley?"

Steve turned to Chris. "Did you kill her?"

Jack interrupted. "Don't answer that."

"What about Sandi? She was with you, Chris. Did she kill Cleo?"

"No.

Steve then pivoted to face Sandi. "And you, Sandi? Did you kill Cleo Stanley?"

"No."

"Did Dr. Chris?"

"It was an accident. Dora accused Chris of giving her fake numbers. They argued. Dora was furious. We all moved to the showroom and the argument turned physical. Dora pushed Chris into Cleo. She was working near the center work station with those silly headphones on."

"Finally, I'm hearing the truth," said Steve.

"No, you're not!" shouted Dora. "He pushed me into that old cleaning lady."

Steve ignored the outburst. "Sandi, what time did this take place?"

"Chris and I arrived a little after midnight and left at twelve thirty in the morning."

"Are you sure?"

"Yes."

"Did you lock the front door after you and Dr. Chris left?"

"Of course. I wouldn't leave Dr. Melody's store open."

"Did Dora leave before or after you?"

"Everyone stayed long enough to make sure Cleo was all right, then, we left together."

The room stayed quiet until Dr. Melody asked, "Are you saying Cleo's death was an accident?"

Steve shook his head. "It might seem like it, but the actions of Dora, Chris, and Sandi all contributed to Cleo's death. Dora planned to obtain a copy of Dr. Melody's records without her permission. Chris wanted to replace them with records of his making. None of them had permission to be there."

Steve faced Sandi. "One last thing. Describe for us exactly what happened to Cleo."

She sat with hands folded on her lap. "Dora followed Chris out of the back office, cussing and threatening him. He had to push her off. He turned and she kicked him square in the back. Chris slammed into Cleo while she vacuumed the carpet by the center workstation. She had her headphones on, and couldn't hear the commotion behind her."

Steve spoke in a soft voice, "What happened then?"

"Everything stopped. The last thing any of us wanted to do was hurt Cleo."

Tears coursed down Sandi's cheeks. "Cleo said she'd be all right. The cut didn't hardly bleed."

Steve turned to Detective Hall. "I believe the next line in this play is yours."

Heather led Steve to a spot away from the door as the detective opened it and motioned for the officer waiting outside to come in.

Once the officer arrived, Hall pointed at Dora Chen and Sandi Fields. "Put those two in cuffs, and take them to jail. I'll take Dr. Chris."

Detective Hall addressed everyone else. "I'll need written statements from everyone. Call me tomorrow morning by nine and I'll set up times."

Chris turned to Jack. "I'll need you to come downtown and help me make bail."

Jack gave his head a side-to-side wag. "You're on your own. I took to heart what they said about enabling people with addictions."

Heather leaned into Steve. "You'll need to find your own way home, too. Tomorrow morning you and I will have a meeting to discuss what you know about ticket stubs to a Boston Red Sox game."

Steve's Adam's apple went up and came back down.

30

S teve awoke the next morning with a sense of dread. After a shower and shave, he dressed for a day in his condo. The first thing on his agenda was coffee, followed by a phone call to Kate. If he didn't call soon with a report of last night's arrests, he'd have two women after his scalp.

He wasn't sure if she'd be busy writing, so he sent a text. "Closed case last night. Call for details."

His phone rang before he had a chance to finish his first cup of the morning. Kate spoke in a hurried sentence. "Start talking, detective, and don't leave out a single detail."

For the next forty-five minutes, that's what he did. It would have taken him fifteen, but the writer needed details. It reminded him of some of his encounters with attorneys for the defense when he was a cop. Answers followed questions, only to give birth to other questions.

Kate's tone went from excitement to elation after he finished. "It's a great ending for the story."

"It may not be as perfect as you think. There's a world of difference between an arrest and a conviction. To begin with, the charges will likely be reduced to manslaughter. It's going to be hard to prove any of them intended to harm Cleo. Dora's in the most trouble, but she also has the most money to spend on attorneys.”

“Stop! A mystery ends when the guilty go to jail. Everything that happens after the arrest is boring. All that’s left to do is tie up loose ends.”

“I still have so much to learn about writing a good story.” Steve scratched his head. “Melody spoke with Heather after Detective Hall took Chris to jail last night. They decided it would be best for Chris to experience some financial pain for his shenanigans. One of Heather’s attorneys will handle Chris’s bankruptcy proceedings.”

Excitement filled Kate’s voice. “A nice touch of resolution. I can use that.”

Steve wasn’t convinced, but he decided to bow to Kate’s expertise as other matters pressed in on his thoughts. “I hope you’re right about the ending, but that’s the least of my worries. Heather found ticket stubs for the Red Socks game. She’s coming over in a while. You might hear her hollering if you stick your head outside.”

“It serves you right for trying to play Cupid.”

“I’m selling my bow and arrows.”

The phone went silent so Steve said, “I’d better go ask Max for advice.”

Kate replied with, “And I need to pull a heroine out of the way of a runaway horse and carriage.”

The phone went dead.

Max settled himself on Steve’s lap and received his usual ration of strokes and head scratches. “I’ve messed up this time, my furry friend. Did Heather tell you what a bad boy I’ve been? No?” Steve huffed. “It’s a good thing. I’m not sure you’re old enough to hear the words I’m due.”

A yawn was the only reply from Max.

“She must have forced Jack to talk. What do you think she used to pry the story out of him? Water-boarding? The bright light in the eyes? A truth serum?” Steve took a drink from his mug. "What's that? You don't think she needs to do any of those things? You're probably right. Women have a way of knowing when something isn't right, and we both know Heather is a special woman. If I lose her help with these cases that keep popping up, I'll be like a cat with its whiskers cut off."

Max stood and arched his back, as if he understood and didn't like the mental image of shears snipping off his whiskers.

"Sorry, old friend. I'll try to come up with a different simile next time." Steve thought for a few seconds. "If there is a next time. I may have burned my last bridge with her." He took another sip. "I still can't believe she made me find my own way home last night."

Max received a dozen more strokes. "Of course, I found a ride. Dr. Melody brought me home. She told me I deserve whatever I get for pretending to be a matchmaker. For a minute, I thought she'd stop the car and tell me to get out. All that talk about deceit and outright lies was fresh in her mind, and she wasn't too happy with men."

Steve kept stroking Max. "Can't say that I blame her. I laid all that talk about deception on thick in order to get confessions. Detective Hall did a good job, too. Did you know cops don't have to tell the truth when they're interviewing a suspect? It works, too."

He closed his eyes. "I might be a hypocrite, but I got to the truth."

Steve lifted his chin. "I hear Heather in the kitchen next door. It won't be long before she tears a large chunk out of my backside. You'd better hide under my bed."

HEATHER COVERED A YAWN. PERHAPS AFTER TODAY, SHE'D GET back to a normal routine. She shook her head. Normal didn't come close to describing her life up to now. She smiled. And with any luck, she'd continue down the path of adventures and surprises.

She walked barefoot to Steve's and banged on the door harder than necessary.

"Come in, Heather," came the reply.

She walked to where he sat in his chair. "Put Max down and join me at the table."

"Have you had coffee yet?"

"We need to talk."

She preceded him to the table and sat in her usual place, facing him. He settled as she made her first accusation. "Why is it you think you can interfere in my personal life?"

"I apologize," he said in a sheepish voice. "I was trying to help."

"Did you ever think I might be like you and not want any help?" She let out a loud huff. "You can start by making a full confession." She waited several seconds before saying, "Well? I'm waiting."

Steve rubbed his hands together, buying time to find a good starting place. He began with slow, deliberate sentences. "The idea to get you and Jack to make a commitment started swirling around in my mind a long time ago."

"How long?"

"Four homicide cases. That includes the one we finished last night."

Heather all but spit out the words. "You've been playing matchmaker since we went to Marble Falls?"

"Yeah. I saw the change come over your father and mother when they came down, met Jack, and approved of him. Then there was the trip to Belize. When we split up and you and Jack went your own way for a few days, something changed in your relationship with him. Admit it, you experienced more than a wonderful vacation."

Heather had to hand it to Steve. He'd read her like a professional poker player reads a novice opponent. She straightened her posture. "Even if that's true, it's our lives, not yours."

"That's not exactly accurate," he countered. "You came back, and we solved that case. Then you immediately got involved with a deal your father cooked up involving a bullet train. You jumped into that project with both feet. Another murder case fell in our laps. That left you trying to please your father, wanting to pursue your relationship with Jack, and helping me solve what turned out to be two murders. No one can do that much. Not even you. So... after that case ended and the rail project fell through, I thought it would be a good time to nudge you in Jack's direction."

"Nudge?" said Heather. "Conspiring with Jack and Father to all but drag me to the altar is your idea of a nudge?"

Steve hung his head. "Jack must have ratted me out about everything. I told Max as much."

Heather had to bite her lip, but she pushed on. "My father filled in the gaps Jack omitted. I have to admit, the timing of this conspiracy was impeccable. You three waited until I was at my most vulnerable."

"That wasn't the original plan. I'll admit it was my idea for you and Jack to go to Boston where your dad would throw Jack out because he didn't measure up. Then, you'd have to choose between the two most important men in your life. Both of your parents liked my plan."

"Wait! Are you saying Mother and Father both approved of this hare-brained scheme?"

"That's why your father pushed ahead with it. He said it was one of your mother's dying wishes that you not push yourself until you turned into a lonely, old woman." Steve paused. "Neither your father nor Jack told you about that, did they?"

Heather had to clear her throat before she could whisper, "I didn't know Mother and Father liked Jack that much."

"Like is too weak a word for what your mother thought of him, and what your father still thinks."

Heather couldn't speak, so Steve continued on. "The timing may have been wrong, and our methods were heavy-handed and clumsy, but we all believed we were pushing you in a direction you wanted to go."

Heather slid her left hand toward Steve. "Take my hand. It's in front of you on your right side."

Steve's fingers inched across the table until their fingertips touched. He pushed his hand a little farther and his smile threatened to show every tooth in his head. "That's a very nice engagement ring."

"You should know. Jack told me you went with him to pick it out."

They squeezed each other's hand. "By the way," said Steve, "your father wants to buy you that catamaran so you and Jack can sail to Belize on your honeymoon. This time, don't argue with him."

"Is there anything about my life you haven't discussed with Father?"

"We only talk about the important things."

"I guess that will be Jack's job from now on."

Steve shook his head. "You're a complicated woman. It'll take all three of us to keep up with you."

Heather came to Steve's side of the table, bent down, and planted a kiss on his cheek. "I wouldn't have it any other way, but don't count on any sudden changes in my marital status. It may take me years to teach Jack how to sail."

MISTLETOE, MALICE AND MURDER

Nothing takes a detective's mind off Christmas like a murder.

Embroiled in a generations-long feud, an oil baron is convinced someone in his family will die soon—and it will probably be him. When blind PI Steve Smiley is called in to find answers, it seems like the perfect opportunity to avoid another bleak Christmas.

After a body is discovered in the tycoon's home, the man is convinced someone's picking off his family one by one. With the clock ticking and the feuding families closing ranks against Smiley, the wily detective must get creative with his investigation.

As he digs deeper, generations of intrigue rise to the surface. Lies and coverups swirl around him like snowflakes. Can Smiley stop the killer before he strikes again, or will this be one case he can't put a bow on?

Scan above to get your copy or go to
brucehammack.com/books/mistletoe-malice-and-murder/

Thanks for reading *Vision of Murder.* I hope it satisfied your appetite for a good mystery and kept you turning the pages to find out 'whodunit.' I would be very grateful if you would take a minute to leave a review at your favorite retail site, Bookbub or Goodreads. Your review could be the one that helps a reader find their next mystery!

To stay abreast of Smiley and McBlythe's latest adventure, and all my book news, join my Mystery Insiders community. For your convenience you may scan the image below. As a thank you, I'll send you a *reader exclusive* Smiley and McBlythe mystery novella.

You can also follow me on Amazon, Bookbub and Goodreads to receive notification of my latest release.

Happy reading!
Bruce

Scan above to sign up or go to brucehammack.com/the-smiley-and-mcblythe-mysteries-reader-gift/

About the Author

Drawing from his extensive background in criminal justice, Bruce Hammack writes contemporary, clean read detective and crime mysteries. He is the author of the popular Smiley and McBlythe Mysteries, the Fen Maguire Mystery series, the Star of Justice series and the Detective Steve Smiley Mysteries. Having lived in eighteen cities around the world, he now lives in the Texas hill country with his wife of thirty-plus years.

Follow Bruce on Bookbub and Goodreads for the latest new release info and recommendations. Learn more at brucehammack.com.